THE
PAGAN TREE

JJ DOBOR

An imprint of Daisy's Blushes Press

info@daisysblushes.co.uk

First published 2021

Cover design by Platform House Publishing

Proofreading by In The Detail

Formatting by Evenstar Books

Print: ISBN 978-1-8384763-0-4

eBook: ISBN 978-1-8384763-1-1

For Rob and my children, with all my love

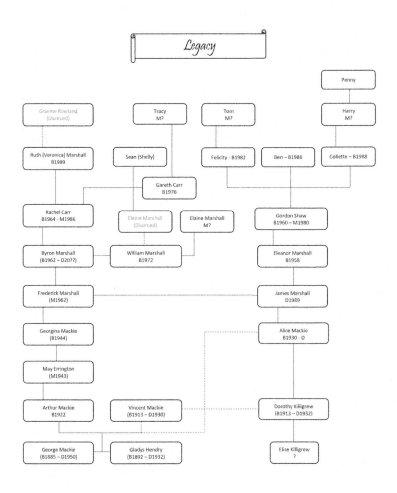

Legacy

Penny

Graeme Rowland
(Divorced)

Tracy
M?

Tom
M?

Harry
M?

Ruth (Veronica) Marshall
B1989

Sean (Shelly)

Felicity - B1982

Ben – B1986

Coliette – B1988

Gareth Carr
B1976

Rachel Carr
B1964 - M1986

Elaine Marshall
(Divorced)

Elaine Marshall
M?

Gordon Shaw
B1960 – M1980

Byron Marshall
(B1962 – D20??)

William Marshall
B1972

Eleanor Marshall
B1958

Frederick Marshall
(M1962)

James Marshall
D1989

Georgina Mackie
(B1944)

Alice Mackie
B1930 - D

May Errington
(M1943)

Arthur Mackie
B1922

Vincent Mackie
(B1913 – D1930)

Dorothy Killigrew
(B1913 – D1932)

George Mackie
(B1885 – D1950)

Gladys Hendry
(B1892 – D1932)

Elise Killigrew
?

CHAPTER 1

THERE'S SOMETHING ABOUT A STRANGE NEW PLACE, the unexpected resonance, nuances and scents, the touch of a breeze, the unfamiliar reflection of light. Excitement and novelty forges the misconception of opportunity, the possibility of a new beginning, a second chance. A place where small findings feel like great discoveries.

My great discovery, and second chance, loomed before me, the refurbished mill the most imposing structure I'd come across in the parish, distance from civilisation, considerable. My mother would hate everything about my new life, not quite my intention, but an added bonus.

The hamlet's focal point was the crossroads. Church and pub faced one another from opposite corners, a cluster of houses flanked the graveyard, and apart from my house and a handful on the adjacent road, nothing but trees and farmland extended as far as the eye could see.

Sunshine glared off the whitewashed walls but offered little warmth. I tucked my hands into my armpits and clenched my gut, dying for a pee after sitting on the motorway for four hours. I climbed the shallow steps to my new front door and resisted the urge to lift the brass handle, looped through the mouth of an ornate lion's head, and knock.

My estate agent, Connie, stylish in a business suit and chiffon blouse, teetered on the edge of the driveway and extended a bunch of keys which dangled from a branded keyring. I wrapped my hand around the cluster of keys and slid a new brass key labelled 'Mill' into the old fashioned keyhole. I expected the lock's wards to resist but the key turn was smooth and the door clicked open.

My heart fluttered. I wished Connie would quit skulking and bugger off so I could wallow in my excitement. I wanted to throw my head back and shout a gleeful "yes" at the sky.

She hesitated at the bottom step and handed me a folder she'd been nursing. "Everything you need to know about the house and appliances is in the pack. You'll need to turn on the heating and hot water." Her eyes flicked to the upstairs windows. "Is there anything else before I leave, Ms Rowland?"

I flipped the folder's cover and peered inside. "No thanks, I'll give you a call if there's anything."

Connie beat a hasty retreat and left me on the threshold. I soaked up the silence and the atmosphere, and hugged my arms against the cold, though sunlight beamed through the front windows and cast bright squares on the floor's polished wood.

Situated at the house's rear, behind the staircase and beyond the sunshine's reach, the kitchen felt utilitarian and bland, and stank of bleach. I dropped the folder onto the worktop and wrinkled my nose. I located the central heating boiler and fiddled with the controls. The unit's internal system erupted and pipes and radiators clicked as they warmed.

Out the corner of my eye I caught a movement outside and leaned on the windowsill to scan the yard. Nothing but the naked branches of a magnolia tree stirred within the boundary walls, and beyond, in the woods, spots of sunshine moved between tangled undergrowth.

With time to spare before my belongings arrived, I explored cupboards and nooks upstairs and wandered through the lounge and dining room, combined to form a capacious and airy space. White walls reflected sunbeams. Pretty chandeliers adorned the ceiling and sunken spotlights lined the kitchen and lit the staircase.

I ran my fingertips along windowsills and the built-in bookshelf's smooth beech shelves. My imagination furnished the house in exaggerated perfection, positioned my things how I wanted them, uncorrupted by someone else's judgement and negativity. My body pulsed with self-satisfaction. I could do this.

The church bell clanged two beats as I shut the door on the departing removal van and faced the stack of boxes which lined the wall. The room smelled of cardboard and dust and my scattered possessions absorbed the house's empty echo.

I cut through the dining area and climbed the cluttered stairs to the large front room I'd chosen for my bedroom. I kicked off my shoes, flopped on the bed, and lay spread-eagled to watch branch skeletons slow dance across the ceiling and walls. I closed my eyes and relaxed into the mattress's softness.

A series of gentle taps woke me. I edged forward on the bed and slid my feet into my shoes. I wasn't in the mood for human interaction, or genial conversation and endless cups of tea. And whatever else country people did. Borrow eggs and sugar. Gather in barns and worship the devil.

A loud bang rattled the front door.

"Keep your socks on." I took the stairs two at a time, cursing whoever hammered on my door. I navigated boxes, adorned my best insincere smile, and opened the door. A gust of wind lifted the ends of my hair. I squinted into the glint of afternoon sun reflected off my car's windscreen.

"Hello?" No reply. Not a soul in sight. I closed the door and followed the draft through to the kitchen. The back door stood open and the stark room felt cold and hostile. I shut and locked the door and tested the handle.

Dawn shone bright beyond the unadorned bedroom window. I pummelled my pillow and chased receding fragments of a dream. The house's thick walls muted outside sounds and I lay, eyes closed, and listened to the silence. Every nerve end tingled. Anxiety had always been my natural waking state. At least as far back as I could remember. As a child I had been a nail biter, and I'd chewed the ends of my hair. I'd grown out of those habits but developed other more harmful behaviours which were harder to break.

I pressed my fingertips into my eye sockets, massaged the puffy flesh and smoothed away fresh tears as they oozed between my eyelashes. Now or never. I propelled myself out from beneath my warm cocoon, tiptoed across the passage to the bathroom, and squealed as my toes touched the bathroom's icy tiles.

I perched on the cold toilet seat, unravelled a handful of toilet paper, and blew my nose. From the showerhead, a cascade of water drops splatted into the bath. I glanced down and recoiled. A twisted heap of my clothes lay submerged in the half-filled tub. A different kind of chill touched my spine and crept over my scalp. I released the plug and watched the water drain from the soggy mound.

At midday I leaned against the kitchen doorframe and downed a cup of tea. I'd spun and dried my clothes, set up the television, and unpacked, washed and stacked crockery, cutlery and sets of glassware Graeme and I had received as wedding gifts, but had never used. Flat packed boxes leaned against the wall, and on the floor at the room's centre I'd accumulated a mound of discarded newspaper and bubble wrap.

Several times throughout the day I found myself upstairs in the bathroom staring at the bath and turning the taps open and closed. I had no memory of stacking my clothes into the bath. And no one but myself to blame for drowning them.

I heard voices outside moments before the knocker tapped. I wiped my hands on my leggings and opened the door. A man, broad as a bison, and a petite woman with a crown of copper hair, grinned at me.

"Hello, there," the woman said, emerald eyes wide with interest as she cast an eye over me. "We meant to drop by last night but something came up."

"Hi, I'm Veronica." I extended an arm, expected to shake hands, and instead got handed a cake tin. I took a step back and smiled. "Please, come inside."

My guests needed no encouragement. "Oh my," the woman said, "the room is so light and airy."

"We thought we'd stick our heads in and say welcome," the man said. He stood beside me whilst the woman roamed through the dining room and into the kitchen. His elbow nudged mine. "I'm Tom, by the way. The inquisitive one is my wife, Felicity."

"Nice to meet you both," I said.

"We haven't seen inside since it's been finished," Felicity said. "Ben's done a fab job with the renovation."

In unison, Tom and I stepped forward and aimed for the kitchen where Felicity stood propped against the worktop looking out the window. I offered tea, gathered mugs and worked as they assessed my yard.

"They've cut the woods back," Felicity said. "You can see the mill ruin now."

Tom hummed and leaned into her back. I joined them and examined the ruin's rusted steel door and paneless window frame. I owned a ruin. The wheelhouse had been overgrown when I'd viewed the property in the summer so I was seeing it for the first time. The house's whitewash ended where the ruin conjoined, a peculiar jagged contour which pointed to the sky. Weeds poked between the rubble of fallen masonry, and bushes and vines snaked between and around charred and blackened beams within the derelict structure.

"We hoped they'd restore it, but I reckon it would cost too much." Tom said, his hand on his wife's bottom. "We've seen photos of before, with the wheel and all. Pity. The guy who had the place before you had big ideas but halfway through remodelling he did a runner. He paid Ben to finish the house off and then put the place back on the market."

"There was a lot of interest," Felicity said. "Londoners wanting a country cottage. The downside is it's the middle of nowhere and there's nothing for kids to do around here. One lot wanted to expand and turn it into a bed and breakfast."

Tom clapped a hand over his mouth. "Oh yeah. Kenver was less than keen on that idea. He's got The Old Mill pub down the road. Not one for competition, is he?"

Felicity gave a slow nod. "He caused ructions with the agent. Lucky for everyone the prospective buyers weren't up for the fight. The owner dropped the price, and here you are."

Here I am.

Connie had omitted quite a lot of detail from her sales pitch. I sliced Felicity's cake, moist chocolate sponge topped with icing and Maltesers, and filled the mugs. I licked icing off my fingers. "I think it's perfect."

"Of course you do," Felicity said. "You bought the place after all. It helps when you like where you're at."

"Yeah, I do like where I'm at."

A look passed between husband and wife. They sipped their drinks and chewed in silence. Tom caught my eye and raised his eyebrows, he smiled and the corners of his eyes wrinkled. "You don't sound like a Cornish girl."

"No, I'm a northern lass." I bit down on my bottom lip.

"Ah, Newcastle?" Tom nodded, his pleasure at sussing my accent obvious by his grin.

I sucked on a Malteser and examined the crumbs on my plate.

Felicity slapped his belly. "You're so nosey." She smiled at me. "The other reason we came by is to invite you to dinner. You know, introduce you to the gang." She formed finger quotes in the air to emphasise her gang.

My insides cramped.

"Will you come? Our place is the last outpost before the caravan park."

Tom folded his arms across his barrel chest. "It's walking distance if you cut through the churchyard."

The thought of socialising with a bunch of strangers who'd judge me and gossip the minute I turned my back sickened me. "Yes, of course," I said. Twenty-something divorcees never made a comfortable social fit. At least not in the society I'd endured all my life.

Felicity beamed. "Fab, how about Friday night? Say seven?"

Five days. More than enough time to concoct an excuse.

Pleasantries over, I provided them with a cursory tour of upstairs before I ushered my visitors down the front stairs and onto the driveway. I shut the door, pressed my forehead to the wood and took several deep breaths.

From the lounge window's recess I watched them amble across the road. Felicity clung to Tom's arm, her slight frame dwarfed by his bulk, the two of them in step, companionable and easy with one another. They seemed nice and I liked their easy manner, but their blatant intrusion unsettled me. I'd relocated five hundred miles to the middle of nowhere to be invisible, to give myself space and time to lick my wounds. Time to heal.

Behind me, a sudden draught ruffled and displaced scraps of paper and wrapping from the stack of discarded packaging and sent them skittering across the kitchen floor.

CHAPTER 2

MY MOBILE PHONE'S SCREEN LIT, and the device vibrated. I placed my glass on the table and answered.

"You promised you'd call." My mother, Rachel Marshall, social climber, psychopath.

"I called the house. You didn't answer," I said. White lie.

"Why would you call the landline? I only keep the thing for the broadband."

I laughed. One day my mother would realise she didn't need a landline to have broadband and then I'd have no backup excuse for not phoning.

"How did the move go?" She exhaled a long breath.

"You said you'd given up smoking."

"I have. I've got a vape thingy. Not a very sophisticated contraption so I puff when no one's around. Don't change the subject."

"The move's work in progress. My stuff's here and I'm unpacking."

"When will you let me know where 'here' is?"

I squeezed my eyes shut. "Let me get settled first. I told you, I need time and space."

"You need to grow up. Graeme's on the phone every day asking about you. What in God's name do you think you're doing?"

I pinched the bridge of my nose. "You're supposed to be on my side, Mother. How am I the one in the wrong?"

"You had everything going for you. Nice house. Money. Holidays. You didn't have to lift a finger."

"You realise how shallow you sound, don't you?" I snatched the glass, gulped a mouthful of wine, and grimaced.

"You've hardly given things a chance. Three years is nothing. I stuck by your father for eighteen years. Sacrifice, sweetheart."

My fingers made blah, blah motions. "And you hated each other and made my life hell. Graeme's priorities are his patients, his social circle and his women. He doesn't give a shit about me. Can we not talk about this?"

"What else is there to talk about? Everyone's talking about it. And everyone thinks I know more than I do. It's bloody frustrating. I'm a fricking celebrity though. All of a sudden everyone wants to talk to me. Even Melinda Cawthorne's invited me to lunch, so give me something to talk about, will you?"

"I'll call you when I'm settled, okay?"

"Don't take too long. I'm worried about you Roo."

Forsaking all semblance of maturity, I performed a silent scream. "Love you too, mum. Speak soon." I ended the call before she could utter another word.

I slumped on the sofa, cradled my glass and stared out the window. Across the room something scraped across the floor. I sat upright and small pink florets bloomed where wine drops slopped on my t-shirt. I scanned the layers of flat packed boxes which propped open the guest toilet door, and searched the floor. Beneath the dining table lay a rectangle of cardboard, small as a postcard.

I shifted a chair and gave the cardboard a toe nudge. The upstairs landing creaked. Walls and corners encroached, and a chill settled on my shoulders like an icy shawl. Blood thrummed in my ears. "Hello?" My voice pitched itself a few octaves short of hysteria.

I plucked the cardboard off the floor and studied the brown corrugated normalness. I blinked back tears. Don't do this Veronica. The move's excitement had masked but not eradicated the bone weariness which had become a constant deep ache. My mother's call had reinforced my misery and paranoia.

I stomped into the kitchen and flung the cardboard into the bin, filled the kettle and tossed a teabag into a mug, the taste of wine sour on my tongue.

Behind me the door clicked and swung open.

For an isolated country pub, the Old Mill bustled with ramblers and tourists, and a handful of locals huddled in their self-allocated spots at the bar, heads bowed, fingers curled around their glasses. Low ceiling beams strung with tankards and walls adorned with sepia prints and brass bric-a-brac gave the interior a cosy feel.

The glow of lighting and warmth from the fire made the room snug. I secured a table, claimed the seat before the departing ramblers' teacups touched their saucers, and studied the menu.

Nobody paid me attention, or looked across and whispered behind their hands as I placed my order at the bar. I sipped my drink, glanced at my mobile phone's dark screen, and fidgeted with my new keyring. I had nowhere else to be, no pressure to impress anyone. The liberating sense of freedom made me giddy.

"Pan fried Cornish hake with salad?" The waitress arrived and cleared space for my plate.

"Thanks. Can I get salt and pepper?"

"Sweetie, you can have whatever you want." She sashayed to the next table and fetched a set of shakers. "Holidaying somewhere local?"

Our eyes connected and my cheeks flushed. "No."

"I'm Shelly." Twentyish, husky voice, fake tan, auburn curls and spider lashes. She folded her arms across her chest and gave a glossy grin. "I haven't seen you around here before."

"I've just moved in, down the road."

Shelly's eyes narrowed and her smile widened. With a dramatic stage whisper she said, "Not the mill house?"

"Yes." Great. Cue all the gossipers, Veronica's in town.

"Oh. My. God." Shelly clapped and did a twirl.

Her shift ended at one. She cleared my table, tugged a cardigan over her uniform and flopped into the opposite chair clutching a pint of lager. "So, what on earth brings you to the wild south west?"

She was easy company and I fed her practiced basics but steered clear of any detail about myself. She reciprocated with a car crash version of her life story as we polished off a bottle of the establishment's finest damson vodka liqueur and several hours later stumbled onto the street arm in arm, two sheets to the wind.

A bank of cloud rolled across the sky and obliterated the morning sun. I stood admiring my bookshelves, hands on hips, pleased I'd finished unpacking. Not a bad effort considering mine and Shelly's impromptu drinking session, and a night wasted sleeping off the effects. My head throbbed and my shoulders and backside ached.

I slid a finger through the fine dust coating the dining table's aquamarine glass top. The chandelier's filtered light gave the base and chairs beneath an underwater effect. I cherished the set almost as much as Graeme had detested it.

I had to stop dwelling on the past, stop associating old memories to my new life. I had to start living, Ms Rowland, no-longer-miserable antisocial ex-wife of easy-on-the-eye Dr Graeme Rowland, all-round ladies' man and mega knobhead.

Three years of marriage, of which the first six months had been the bliss of dreams, had left me wounded, the sting of rejection a constant reminder of my failure to keep hold of my husband. My mother blamed me for his philandering. Woe me, the faithful and adoring sop, so infatuated I couldn't see past his ugliness?

I had dressed the part, behaved as expected, yet always got abandoned at parties and functions whilst others whispered about me. Often enough they hadn't bother to whisper, their words well-aimed arrows pitched to wound.

I took the stairs two at a time and glanced into the bathroom as I passed. The tub lay vacant.

The rear bedroom contained my office paraphernalia and a stack of boxes marked bedroom and general excess. A calendar alert on my phone reminded me I had an article deadline and spurred me to action. I salvaged what I needed, settled on my bed, and worked into the evening. The sky turned yellow-grey to ash, then bruised slate to night. No city lights or streetlamps marred the starry blackness.

The tulip leaf lampshade cast hoop shadows around my bedroom ceiling, and semi-darkness cloaked the corners. Clothing and makeup covered the bed. Every drawer lay open and cupboard doors gaped, awaiting their stash.

Above the light fitting, something metallic dropped, rolled across the ceiling and stopped near the wardrobe.

My heart pounded against my ribs. Something scratched around, then feather light steps tiptoed across the ceiling's expanse. The wood creaked until the footsteps faded.

I held my breath and fought a stab of panic. "Who's there?" I waited. Seconds felt like minutes. There had to be a logical explanation. Didn't there? Tiptoeing rats. Big bloody rats. I pounded across the hallway and down stairs, seized the remote control and turned on the television. Any sound was better than gravid silence.

Satisfied, I climbed the staircase, turned at the mid landing and stopped. Primal terror riveted me to the floor and a rash of goose bumps flushed over my skin. I glanced over the handrail at the dining table. At its centre, beneath the chandelier's trembling crystal drops, sat a glass of water.

A moan rose in my throat as the tinkling crystals shot a kaleidoscope of prisms against the walls and ceiling. The light blinked out and the prisms shot off into the inky darkness. An advert jingle played out on the television screen. Blue-tinged shadows flashed against the windows' oily glass.

The temperature plummeted. Darkness congealed around me and the acrid fetor of wood smoke filled my nostrils. Frigid fingers touched my cheek and caressed my neck and collarbone, traced a path from shoulder to elbow and touched my hand.

"*Roo . . .*" Invisible lips whispered a breath of cold air into my ear. I screamed and fell to the floor clawing at my face as my fingers raked through cobwebs of frosty hair.

The television's speakers warbled the first bars of a familiar theme tune and a woman's voice introduced the programme's location. I lay on the floor gasping, arms shielding my face, knees tucked into my chest. Warmth flooded the room, but I couldn't bring myself to open my eyes and look.

Time passed and the floor became uncomfortable. I uncurled and sat, opened my eyes and kept them trained on my knees until I was certain nothing horrendous lurked beyond my peripheral vision.

The chandelier burned bright, expelled all shadows, the crystal drops motionless on their transparent threads. The glass of water reflected the light above.

I got to my feet, wrapped my arms around myself, and looked around. Except for the glass, everything appeared normal. I slunk down the stairs and towards the table and lifted the glass. The water was smooth and still, and frozen solid.

I ran to the kitchen and dropped it into the sink. My face reflected stark against the dark window. Before any apparition had time to materialise I cleared the distance to the hallway and scaled the stairs like I had a demon on my tail.

I woke. Rain pattered against the windowpanes. I propped myself on an elbow and looked around the room. The door remained shut, a flimsy barrier between me and my psychosis.

I checked the time on my mobile phone. A missed call notification and a text from my editor exacted an expletive. I touched the cold radiator. Nine o'clock and no heating. I let out a heavy sigh. One way or another, I had business with Connie and her heating engineer.

One way or another, I had to face what awaited me beyond my bedroom door.

CHAPTER 3

BEN SHAW STOOD ON MY STEPS, six foot something, sandy hair, hazel eyes and week-old stubble, garbed in t-shirt, workman trousers and safety boots. He gave me the once over. "Connie says you're having a spot of bother with the heating."

Pleasantries out the way then. "The boiler seems to be fine. The problem is the radiators. They're all cold."

He stepped past me, walked to the kitchen and examined the boiler and the wall thermostat and felt the radiators and inlet pipes. "There must be air in the system. I'll grab my tools and take a look."

Whilst he worked on the radiators I went upstairs and sorted my clothing into the drawers and wardrobe. A while later he appeared in my bedroom doorway. "I've bled the system and the radiators are getting hot," he said. He slid his hands into his pockets and leaned against the doorframe. "This is my favourite room, lots of light."

His assessment of my bedroom made me uncomfortable. I scanned the bed and floor for stray underwear. "Thanks," I said, "I appreciate you coming to the rescue at such short notice."

"Any time." His smile didn't falter. "Although, according to Connie, I didn't have much choice in the matter."

My cheeks flushed. I'd ranted empty threats at Connie for a good ten minutes.

He sauntered towards the stairs. "I've left my card in the kitchen. Call if you need help with anything."

I failed to connive a reasonable excuse to skip Felicity and Tom's dinner party. Dressed and ready by half past six, I opted to walk the long way round beneath street lights instead of through the unlit churchyard. .

I located their house and Felicity shepherded me inside. The weather had taken a mild turn and wood smoke swirled about the garden and took flight over the wall. So much for dinner. I hated barbecues. Too casual. Too much opportunity for getting personal.

Felicity popped a salad tomato in her mouth. "I hope you don't mind the change of plan. Tom will keep the boys busy with the barbecue and we girls are going to fill you in on all the gossip whilst we get to grips with these babies."

I eyed the line-up of bottles of prosecco, gin and liqueurs. "How much gossip can a hamlet have?"

"You'll be surprised." Felicity opened her mouth, scooped in a handful of peanuts and continued her bumble bee flight around the kitchen. "And you'll find out who's doing what . . . and who."

I laughed. "I've heard about these insidious little communities." Well, Shelly's version at least.

Felicity downed the dregs of her glass. "Sweetie, you have no idea."

The doorbell sounded and Tom vanished. I took a slow ragged breath to calm my nerves. Ben walked into the kitchen, clean shaven and nicely packed into t-shirt and jeans. He thrust a bouquet of supermarket flowers into Felicity's arms and kissed her on the forehead.

"Benjie, this is Veronica. Veronica, my brother Ben."

"We've met," Ben said. "Heating incident at the mill." He snatched a wedge of pâté coated bread and stuffed it in his mouth.

Felicity frowned. "Problems already?"

He popped the lid off a beer. "Teething problems. Nothing we can't fix." He tapped my glass with the bottle's lip. "Cheers."

The doorbell went again followed by a horde of voices. Ben grinned. "Align your troops."

Felicity gave him a look. She opened the freezer and handed him a bag of ice. "Make yourself useful with the drinks."

Men gathered around the fire, their voices a baritone mumble punctuated by an occasional scoff of laughter. Women hunkered around me competing to impress or intimidate. Felicity spilled more drink than she managed to get into the glasses, already steaming towards a stinking hangover.

"I hear you've had our Ben all to yourself today." Elaine spoke, upward of fifty, too much make-up, and garish blonde hair. Mutton-dressed-as-lamb.

"You lucky cow." Tracy chipped in, tall, thirty-something, cropped black hair, crafted nails, tight white trousers and black lace blouse through which poked dark pert nipples.

Felicity made a face and swirled the ice in her drink.

Elaine tilted her glass at my naked hand. "Where's your man?"

Three months since the divorce and I remained manacled by a pale tan line where my rings used to be. "I'd imagine he's posturing at some party or another, getting stuck into a tart or two." I said. God, I sounded like my mother.

Elaine's eyebrows shot up. Tracy spat a mouthful into her glass and laughed.

"Why on earth did you buy the mill," Elaine said. "A young woman like you needs to be in the hub of things, nightlife and hunky men."

"No thanks," I said. "Been there, done that. I've got a mountain of work to keep me busy. I don't need distractions."

"What work do you do?" Tracy said.

"I write. Commissions, articles and stuff."

"Journalist."

"No. I've a degree in journalism, but I'm more a feature writer."

"Same thing."

Shelly sucked on an ice cube she'd clamped between her teeth. "Have you had any more visits from your resident ghost?"

A tonic bottled slipped from Felicity's grasp and hit the table, spilling the contents.

I relished the swift change of subject. "Several, actually."

Elaine chuckled and clinked glasses with Shelly. "What are you like, there's no such thing as ghosts."

"Are too." Shelly scooped and tossed her mass of hair over her shoulders. "Tell them Veronica."

Ben entered the kitchen via the patio door. Shelly hooked a finger under his t-shirt's hem, leaned into him and pushed her breasts against his chest. "Hello big boy."

He blew hair out of his face and elbowed her aside, his eyes on me as he passed through the door into the hall. Elaine smirked at Shelly, who flicked her the middle finger.

Tracy placed her glass on the counter and followed Ben. Felicity downed her drink and turned to make another. Shelly pouted and fiddled with her glass.

"Have one of these." Felicity handed me a blue-tinged cocktail.

I wrinkled my nose. "I'm going to need medical attention if I have any more to drink."

Elaine chuckled. "Sad to say we have no dishy doctors to attend to you this neck of the woods."

"Just old men," Shelly said. Her eyelashes tangled with her fringe and she made a fuss of separating the strands. "There's never any nice guys, just this bunch of fuckwits."

"Dan seems like a pretty decent bloke," I said. All eyes shifted to slim and stylish Dan. He'd come from London to spend the weekend. He and Shelly had history, the type in inverted commas, though unlike the rest of her life story she remained cagey on the detail.

She wiggled her toes, little strawberries in a line-up. "He is, but he's just a friend."

Felicity wound a strand of Shelly's hair around her fingers. "Honey, you can't appreciate the apple's sweetness unless you take a bite."

"You know that's a stupid analogy, don't you?" Shelly said.

Felicity clicked her tongue. "Whatever. Think of Eve in the Garden of Eden. She didn't hesitate to nosh the apple."

I glanced at Tom and considered Felicity's wealth of experience with apple noshing. Mother Teresa giving Madonna sex education.

"So, tell us about the ghost." Elaine flopped an arm around Shelly's shoulder and they focused their attention on me.

Shelly perked and her sulk twisted into a smile.

"Haven't you ladies had enough to drink?" Ben returned to the kitchen with a mussed and glossy-eyed Tracy in tow.

Shelly's eyeballs swivelled into a theatrical roll. "We drink to forget." She turned her back on Tracy and flounced outside. Tracy adjusted her blouse and licked her lips. She disgusted me. I couldn't count the times I'd witnessed Graeme's women do the exact same thing themselves after lengthy absences.

Shelly waved me across to the fireside. She'd positioned herself between Dan and Elaine's husband Bill, which left me sandwiched between Tom and Tracy's husband, Gareth.

"Brave girl taking on the mill," Gareth said. "Or plain bloody stupid."

His snide tone surprised me. "Neither, really. It's a house like any other."

Gareth scoffed. "Not like any other house. Not by a long shot."

Tom winked at me. "Big old house for a young girl, he means."

"Not what I mean, and you know it." Gareth nursed his beer. "That place should have been left alone. It's no place for an outsider."

His words and attitude rankled me. I spied Felicity doling out cocktails and figured I'd be better off rat-arsed with Tracy for company.

"Thanks for the heads up," I said. The firelight flickered in the man's eyes. His head drooped and he inspected his beer bottle's label. "And I might be an outsider to you," I said, "but my family are from here so I've as much right to be here as any one of you lot."

I stacked a pile of plates on the kitchen island and looped the tea towel through the oven handle. Felicity lay head in arms on the table.

Tom kissed her face. "My girl's out for the count. She's going to be teasy as an adder tomorrow."

Ben slapped Tom's arm. "See to her, I'll walk Veronica home."

"There's no need." My response was taciturn and my cheeks flared.

Tom carried Felicity to the sofa and dropped her onto the cushions. He waved us out and shut the door. The light went off and left us in darkness.

A pool of white light snapped on at my feet. "Come on then," Ben said. "Let's get you home." He bounded ahead, his long legs carrying him faster than my wasted ones could manage.

The moonless sky blanketed the churchyard in

shapeless shadows. I stumbled with every step and had to grab hold of Ben to stop myself falling. He curled an arm around my waist and held me against him, warm and sturdy, in control.

When my shoes touched the tarmac beyond the church gate I withdrew, took back control. My house loomed, a brooding hulk against the dark sky.

"I thought I left a light on." I didn't have the strength for another round of Amityville Horror.

"Not to worry," Ben said. "I'll see you in." He pointed the flashlight in my face. I slapped a hand across my eyes, white circles burnt into my retinas. Blinded, I fumbled with my keys. He pried the bunch from my hand and after a couple of attempts unlocked the door. A wave of frigid air engulfed us. "Ah shit, the heating's off," he said, as the house swallowed him.

I kicked the door shut and felt along the wall for the light switch.

"You left your back door open." He shouted from the kitchen.

I'd locked the door. I'd double checked the stupid door. Ben stood on the back step, hands in his pockets. I slid open the cutlery drawer where the key lay in the teaspoon compartment. I handed him the key. "I locked the door before I left."

"Must be a dodgy catch. I'll check it out in the morning," he said.

I tailed him to the lounge, expecting him to leave.

Instead, he flopped onto the sofa, positioned a cushion behind his head and stretched out.

I haggled with myself whether to offer coffee or tell him to go. He had to go. "Ben?"

No answer.

"Shit." I paced the room. I stood and stared at him. I nudged his leg. "Ben?"

I gave up and fetched him a blanket.

Chapter 4

Before my divorce, I'd measured time against work deadlines. Otherwise, days blurred into an abstract watercolour, shapeless, without definition or meaning. My mother had filled the gaps with tedious lunches, endless shopping excursions, and parties. Without those minor distractions, life would have been a whitewash.

The two weeks I'd afforded myself to settle into my new home had flown by. Not a day passed without interruption from one or all my new friends, and incessant phone calls from my mother, eager for clues to my whereabouts. I was being pedantic withholding the detail and knew beyond doubt she'd first inform Graeme, then make a beeline for me.

Thirteen days had passed, in which I'd accommodated two impromptu night guests and a barbeque, several brushes with my supernatural housemate, and more hangovers than I cared for. And the cherry on top of my cake of inhibition? A séance.

Saturday night entertainment came courtesy of Tracy, who commandeered the dining table, and what she termed the 'hexed glass', and set out her homemade Ouija board. My protests went unheard and I found myself a reluctant participant in one of her many power plays.

An hour into the ritual Felicity called for a pit stop to calm her nerves. Shelly belly laughed at the expression on Elaine's face as she pushed her chair back and stood.

"It's not working because it's not a round table." Tracy lifted a violet and crystal dusted nail off the upturned glass's base. "I mean, what shape is this thing anyway?"

"Can we not do this?" Elaine paced the floor, circling the table. "It's dangerous. Veronica has to live in this house, you know."

"She's a big girl, Lainie." Shelly flicked a strand of hair. "Besides, it's the only way we're going to get any ghost action around here. If you keep pacing, there's no chance we'll get a visitation."

"Shut up, Shelly," Elaine said. She squeezed my shoulder as she passed behind my chair. "It's your big gob that's chased it away."

Tracy straightened the paper letters and numbers and repositioned the candles at each end of the table. "Sit Elaine, let's try again. It's not going to work if you don't take it seriously."

Shelly and Elaine flopped into their chairs and

clasped one another's hands. Tracy extended one hand towards me, and Felicity took hold of her other hand to complete the circle.

"Now hold tight," Tracy said. "Feel the room around you, open your mind to the whole house."

Elaine's eyes grew big and frightened. Shelly pursed her mouth to quash a smile.

"Spirit of Mill House, are you here?"

Five nervous pairs of eyes swivelled around the room.

"Each place a finger on the glass. Don't push." Tracy let go of my hand and leaned forward, her finger the first to touch the glass. Felicity followed then Shelly and me. Elaine's finger hovered for a second then settled next to mine.

"Spirit of the house, reveal your name."

Nothing.

My breathing sounded loud and unnatural. I shifted in my chair.

The glass moved a millimetre. Elaine whimpered and glared at me. My bladder almost let go.

"Take your time," Tracy said, her eyes closed, lashes dark against her skin.

The glass jerked and slid sideways. Shelly grinned ear to ear, in her element. My arm tingled as the glass paused and made a slow arc before gliding around the table's centre and hesitating at the letter F.

Elaine hyperventilated. The glass jerked into action and spelled out U – C – K and slid to a stop.

Felicity lifted her finger and scowled at Tracy. "Seriously?"

Shelly threw her head back, stamped her feet, and howled at the ceiling. Tracy swept the papers into a pile, scooped them into the glass, and banged it down on the table. "You're a bunch of spoil sports." And to Shelly, "You need psychiatric help."

"You're so last year on that one, babe." Shelly said.

I leaned back and smiled. "You're like a bunch of bored schoolgirls. Tea, coffee, wine? Spirits?"

"Spirits?" Elaine whined, "I have to walk home in the dark, you know."

"When did the dark or being trollied ever stop you?" Tracy followed me to the kitchen and deposited the glass on the counter. I handed her a bottle of peach schnapps and arranged shot glasses on a tray.

Three rounds of schnapps later, Elaine and Shelly ranted about Arthur Mackie, a stick thin octogenarian who took walks in his garden in an unfastened dressing gown and flashed his treasures at anyone he caught looking.

A cool breeze circled my ankles. A chill rose behind me and settled around my shoulders, prickling up my neck. I glanced at the others, but they seemed oblivious. Their voices receded. The frigid air caressed my skin. In the silent void I heard the glass in the kitchen slide across the granite worktop, long stroke, pause, short stroke, short stroke, long stroke, backward and forward across the stone surface.

"Veronica?" Felicity waved a hand in front of me. Their voices exploded in my ears, bickering as if they'd never stopped. I focused on her face, on the fine lines at the corners of her eyes. "You okay?"

I clenched my jaw so hard my teeth ground together. "Yeah, fine." I forced a smile.

"I'm off," Elaine said. She launched herself off the sofa and staggered to the door with her coat in tow. "Who's walking me home?"

Elaine's drunken strolls were a familiar sight on the crossroad at night. I marvelled at the woman's capacity for alcohol and gossip. I hadn't yet become a target for her sundowner visits but imagined my time would come. She was a rough diamond. A familiar loneliness lurked within her.

"Come on you old slag." Shelly looped a hand through Elaine's arm, and they tottered out onto the driveway.

Tracy rifled through her handbag and lifted out her mobile phone. She poked the screen, gave me a dark look, and smirked. "Don't wait up, ladies," she said, "I have to see a man about a dog."

Shelly shot me a look and arched a brow. "See you tomorrow? Lunch at the Old Mill?"

"Twelve thirty. Reserve me a spot near the fire," I said.

I closed the door and turned the key. Their laughter faded into the night. Warmth seeped from the room and I sensed the back door stood open. The lights went out and a wave of fear washed over me.

Oh God, something came towards me. I pressed my forehead against the door. Frosty breath cooled the back of my neck. Cold fingers touched my hand. A scream caught in my throat and I exhaled a plume into the icy air.

Come.

The whisper came from everywhere, and nowhere, across the room, behind me, in my ear. Feather light fingers probed my clenched hand, compelling me to follow. Dark shadows lurked all around me. I couldn't bring myself to turn, terrified of what I might see. I waited. I moved, tentative steps, one foot in front of the other until I stood, shivering, on the back doorstep.

Beneath the starlit sky stood a man, his skin incandescent, eyes dark smudges under a floppy fringe. He wore baggy trousers, a jacket and tie, and clutched a straw boater to his chest. He flickered, like a silent movie playing out on an invisible screen.

Come.

I followed him through a gap behind the mill and into the trees beyond the boundary wall. I glanced back at the house. Lights shone behind every window. Compelled by the apparition's call, I navigated a path I couldn't see. A slight breeze teased the canopy of damp branches and the cloying smell of rotting mulch filled my nostrils.

With each tentative step I kept the man in my sight as he passed through undergrowth and low-hanging boughs, haloed in shimmering sepia, until he stopped, turned, and flickered out of existence.

With no sense of direction, I battled rising panic. I didn't fear the spectre, nor the darkness. I feared the unknown which yawned around me and tormented my senses, the teasing touches and anxious expectation of a fairground tunnel of terror. The static before a thunderstorm.

A gossamer finger touched my cheek, a flutter, cold and damp. Then more fluttering, like a colony of leathery bats, clapping their wings in preparation for flight. I tilted my head a fraction and beheld the starry sky between tangled shadows. Overhead imagined bats morphed into shuddering fragments of black against the cosmic backdrop.

I staggered, toppled backwards and landed on my backside on hard ground. Slimy snakes twisted and slid beneath me. My nails clawed and I grappled for purchase. Blind terror spurred me into a lurching run, but I slipped and fell, and snakes coiled around my ankles and dragged me into the wet, stinking dankness.

I screamed as icy scales slithered against the exposed skin of my neck. Another creature encircled and clamped my ankle. I kicked and my shoeless foot connected with a looming shadow which expelled a tirade of abuse in a deep and familiar voice.

"What the fuck?" I crawled backwards, like an upside-down spider, away from the shadow. I tangled with the snakes and collapsed in a thrashing heap, fear extending beyond the threshold of sanity.

"Who is it?" The voice shouted. The shadow loomed over me. Then threw itself at me and crushed me against the snakes. Its breath reeked of alcohol.

Crazed, and in a haze of terror, I shoved against my attacker. My knee struck soft flesh. The shadow groaned in varying tones of agony then started to laugh and fight back. Strong hands clamped my wrists and his weight settled across me and wedged my legs apart, starving my lungs of air.

I sobbed and gasped. Panic and a lack of oxygen sent my head into a spiral and I slumped on the cold ground, unable to struggle against his strength.

Sunshine. Coffee. The tantalising aroma flavoured the air, blended with the still unfamiliar scent of my new life. I snuggled into the duvet's warmth. My neck hurt. I changed position and groaned at my body's protest. Spears of pain stabbed the muscles in my arms, back and legs.

Memory flashed, like a cold hard slap. I threw back the duvet and scrambled out of bed. My clothes lay in a heap. Dried mud coated my skin and I wore the previous day's panties and bra. I had no recollection of returning home, or undressing. I staggered to the wardrobe and tugged my dressing gown off the hanger, draped it over my shoulders and shoved my arms into the sleeves.

At the top of the stairs I stood and listened. Someone fussed about downstairs. Mugs clinked and a teaspoon tinkled. The kettle rumbled to a boiled, then snapped off. I tiptoed back to bed, slid under the duvet and buried my head in the pillows. I got my breathing under control, lay still, and feigned sleep.

Bare feet patted up the stairs and across the landing and paused at the bedroom door. My heart pounded as they approached the bedside and placed a mug on the bedside table. A rough finger swept strands of hair out of my face. "Wakey wakey, Sleeping Beauty."

CHAPTER 5

BEN CROUCHED BESIDE ME, clutching the mattress edge. He smiled and lines radiated from the corners of his eyes. "Coffee?"

My heart did a double skip. I shuffled into a seated lotus, cocooned myself in folds of duvet and took the offered mug. He limped to the opposite side and flopped onto the bed next to me. The sweet hot coffee soothed both my throat and jangled nerves. I eyed him over the cup's lip.

"Don't panic," he said, his smile teasing, "Your virtue is intact."

"You undressed me?"

He shrugged, "The light was off. I didn't see anything."

Doubtful. "What happened?"

"You tell me. I was heading home from the pub and next thing there's a wriggling, screaming creature rolling around under the rag tree. When I realised it was you I tried to calm you, but you went nuts." He indicated a ridge of scratches crusted with dried blood which extended from his cheek down his neck.

"Oh God, Ben, I'm so sorry." I'd given him a right going over. "What's a rag tree?"

"You first. What were you doing out there in the dark?"

I brushed over the details of Tracy's Ouija session, and described the man I'd followed through the trees, how he'd disappeared, about the bats and snakes. My story sounded ridiculous, alcohol-fuelled and delusional. He listened, sipping his coffee. I expected him to laugh, or at least crack a joke at my expense.

"It wasn't snakes and bats," he said. He squeezed my foot. "Just the rag tree. Your bats are bits of cloth, ribbon, you name it. Snakes," he snorted, "are roots. The ground around the tree is eroded from visitors. The roots are exposed and can be quite treacherous when wet, or in the dark."

"Another detail Connie omitted from her sales pitch."

He raked his fingers through his hair. "I didn't know there existed a path from the house to the tree," he said. "I don't think anyone does."

I placed my empty mug on the table, hugged my knees and buried my face in the duvet. If I carried on like this, I'd be the local laughingstock. Ben leaned against the headboard. From the peephole in the crook of my arm I could see the hairs on his leg and realised he was in his boxer shorts.

"Grab a shower and I'll take you down," he said. "You can show me the path your man took."

I lifted my head. "You're not wearing any pants. Did you stay over?"

He grinned. "Didn't think you'd mind, under the circumstances."

"Where did you sleep?"

"Right here." He patted the bed. "You were spaced out. I got your muddy kit off and gave you a bit of a clean. You slept like a baby." My cheeks and neck burned. He leaned over and slid an arm around me. "It's okay. You're okay."

I twisted out of his grip. "You know nothing about me. I'm not okay. This is not okay." I hated the tone of my voice. He'd brought me home, put me to bed and looked after me.

"Fine. Sorry." He perched on the bed's edge with his back to me.

No. What was I doing? I didn't want him to be sorry. I liked him sitting on my bed, making me coffee. "I could be a crazy nymphomaniac," I said.

He turned, a glint in his eyes. "I can work with that."

"Or a kleptomaniac?"

He laughed. "Are you?"

I curled my fingers into claws. "Or I might be a cannibal."

He looked at me for a long moment. "And eat me?"

Oh God, what did I say? I rolled off the bed and made a beeline for the bathroom. Maybe wash my mouth out with soap. Run a cold shower.

"This way." I called over my shoulder, ducking beneath branches which snagged my hair and t-shirt. The path peeped through grass and brambles and wound under bushes and fallen branches, teasing me along as it disappeared under rotted leaf fall from a long-forgotten summer and reappeared meandering between trees, thorny vines and gorse.

I stopped where the mesh of roots began, twisted woody earthworms burrowing into the mud. The tree, which had loomed monstrous under the night sky, in the milky morning light stood docile on the fringe of the woods. In the branch canopy, flashes of colour danced, bits of fabric, frayed and faded, scarves, knotted and limp with mildew and moisture, ribbons, lace, ties, a sock, a child's teddy suspended by a stained ribbon, a length of police tape wrapped around a branch.

Not a bird sang from the mournful branches. No sound, other than the tree's treasures fluttering and rustling. There existed a sense of wrongness, and sadness. Misery clenched my heart and tears blurred my vision. I choked on a lump of despair, ached for souls lost, and for the faithful fingers which had tied those knots. And wept at the anguish within myself.

Ben touched my shoulder. I didn't pull away, desperate for the comfort of another human being. My skin warmed beneath his hand.

"It's this place," he said, "it does that to you. People come here all the time, some to make wishes, to pray, grieve for loved ones, for lost children." He pointed to the dirty, faded teddy bear, one beady eye long gone, a bit of thread all that remained in a hollow socket.

I had to get away. I picked my way across the roots, searched for the path home.

"Better to follow the road back," Ben said. He took my hand. "It's quicker. And safer."

We walked side by side, hand in hand, elbows rubbing, feet in step though he still had a slight limp. I stared at the ground, trailed the tarmac's rough edge where it met gravel, like a frayed black ribbon winding through the countryside. The church's squat tower came into sight as we rounded a bend and I knew where I was.

We let go hands at the same time. "No need to see me home," I said, my throat clogged with emotion. "Thanks . . . for everything."

"Call me." He squinted against the sun. "Any time."

I turned away as my lip trembled and fresh tears threatened.

I let myself in, relieved to find the house warm. Exhausted, bruised inside and out, and losing my mind,

I had no appetite for drama. I'd left my mobile phone on the bed to charge and tapped the screen. A text from my editor and a missed call from my mother, and less than an hour to get ready for lunch with the gang.

"That old tree's always been there." Elaine sat like a man, an ankle resting on her knee. Cotton Eye Joe blared from the speakers and her foot waggled in time with the beat.

"I've seen something similar in Scotland, near Inverness," Tracy said. Underdressed, as usual, in skin-tight pants and a skimpy top, she sat with her legs stuck straight out in front of her, tapping her boot toes together.

Shelly cleared the dishes from our table and winked as she caught my eye. "Dessert?"

"I'll have a coffee, thanks."

Elaine shook her head. "My mother and I used to take walks to the woods on Sundays. Our special time. We'd natter about everything, set the world to rights," she said. "There wasn't half the amount of traffic in those days." Her eyes lost focus. "I miss her."

"Load of hogwash if you ask me." Tracy lowered her legs and did a seated tap dance. "Mumbo jumbo mush."

"That's a bit harsh," I said. "Imagine all those people who find solace in those places."

She did a raspberry. "Load of shite."

"Everyone from around here has a bit of something

tied in the tree," Elaine said. "There's a teddy for Filly's lost boy."

I recalled the one-eyed teddy dangling from a branch.

"Sticking things on a sodding tree isn't going to bring them back, is it?" Tracy swallowed a mouthful of wine. She twitched, like a cat on a hot tin roof. Like she needed to be somewhere else.

Shelly slid a mug of coffee between my elbows and pulled up a chair. "I'm with Tracy on this."

I studied her face, the swells beneath her eyes. She'd been crying. Everything about her lacked lustre in a dejected non-Shelly kind of way. I fought the urge to invite her back to mine after her shift. I needed respite from these insane women and lacked the capacity for another pity party.

Tracy checked her phone for the hundredth time, irritation wrinkling the spot between her eyebrows. Elaine picked up on the prelude to exit and hoisted herself out of her chair, groaning as she straightened, a hand pressed into the base of her spine. "Best person to speak to about the tree is Father Murphy."

I waved them off, finished my coffee, waited until Shelly disappeared into the kitchen, and left the pub. The church car park stood empty of sinners' cars. Father Murphy stood on the church steps, hands clasped behind his back, cassock flapping in the breeze.

As I approached, he extended an arm and gave my hand a vigorous shake. "Ah, Sleepy Hollow's newest

resident, Veronica is it? Liam Murphy at your service."
He led me around the churchyard and chatted about my
house renovation. We passed a huddle of old ivy-entwined
graves, tended but secluded beneath stark trees.

I answered his countless questions and weaselled
myself into the conversation. "I've been told you're the
go-to guy for information on the rag tree."

"Ah, the clootie well." He nodded. "Yes." He adjusted
his glasses. "A Celtic tradition. Goes way, way back. Pagan
beliefs, ideas of healing, finding love, placing offerings to
spirits and saints alike. There's a few of them in Scotland,
and Ireland too."

"I came across ours last night," I said.

He rocked on his heels. "How come at night then?"

"I . . . went for a walk," I said. Bending the truth to
God's man felt wrong somehow.

"And you found it, in the dark."

"Yes, Father." I broke eye contact, scrutinised a
nearby headstone.

"Well," he said, "now you have its location, you can
visit in the daytime too. Imagine my surprise at finding
one on my doorstep when I was posted to this parish.
I had no idea they extended as far down the country as
Cornwall.

"There's not much evidence of a well, just a small
stone font and a bit of a puddle, but it's an impressive
sight nonetheless."

I bit my treacherous bottom lip. "I've been back this

morning, but didn't like it much. Too sad."

He frowned. "That stretch of the woods has a way of soaking up sadness, my dear, absorbing it through bark and leaf, those rags like bandages to a multitude of wounds. Personally, I don't see the joy in these places. The ground sucks in misery and pain. Folk would benefit more from the Lord's blessings rather than these faithless follies." His jaw clenched. A moment of silence passed between us. "Will you be joining us in worship once you're settled?"

The lie rolled off my tongue like warm butter. "Of course, Father."

CHAPTER 6

HARD TO SAY WHICH STARTLED ME MORE, the thunderous crash upstairs, or the whisper in my ear, "*Roo . . .*"

I lay on the sofa in the dark, heart pounding. The storm had knocked the power out and upstairs a door slammed and wind swept debris down the stairs. I located the light on my phone and felt my way to the banister and managed to climb to the midway landing before retreating beneath a shower of bits of ceiling and branches.

I fumbled with the phone, fingers cold and trembling, and selected Ben's number. After several rings, his sleepy voice barked in my ear.

"Ben?"

"Veronica, you okay?"

"I think a tree's fallen through my roof."

"Where are you?"

"Downstairs."

"Shit. Stay there, I'm on my way."

Within minutes he banged on the door. He and the wind and rain threw themselves inside, almost ripping my arm from its socket. He pocketed his keys and disappeared upstairs. I risked the vortex and waited at the foot of the stairs whilst his torch beam cut through the darkness.

He appeared, his mouth moving but the sound drowned out by the storm's deafening roar. Then he was down, arms around me. "You need to come back to mine. I can't tell the extent of damage in the dark, but if the roof goes the lot could come crashing down on you."

He draped a throw across my shoulders, grabbed my phone and keys off the coffee table, and we made a dash for his van. He gunned the engine, and as we pulled away I saw the felled tree's dark mass protruding from my roof.

Ben's house was compact and cosy, and dry. He lit candles, which cast a warm glow and sent shadows leaping around his lounge, and replaced my damp throw with a blanket. "You can have my bed. I'll sleep down here."

Exhaustion outweighed my concern about where I would sleep, and his sofa was way too small for him to sleep on. "I'll take the sofa." I settled onto the cushions before he could protest.

"The loo's upstairs. Shout if you need anything."

For a long while I lay and listened to the rain lash the windows, my thoughts in turmoil. I dozed and repositioned myself. My arm dangled and my fingers tracked the floor's grain along the sofa's underside. Something snagged my finger and I fiddled with a small plastic oval until sleep claimed me.

"Vee?" Ben touched my shoulder. I stirred, reluctant to face reality. "We need to get over to your house and check the damage," he said, giving me a shake. "Whilst there's a lull in the storm. I've asked Tom to meet us in half an hour."

I groaned and forced my eyes open. He nestled a mug of coffee. I propped myself on an elbow and reached for the mug. A glossy red nail fell from my hand and landed at his feet. A muscle twitched in his jaw. He passed me the coffee and snatched up the nail.

Felicity stood beside me and we watched from across the road as Ben and Tom moved about on the roof and in the breach where the tree had torn a jagged hole. "You can come and stay at ours," she said, her neck craned as she watched Tom toss branches into the garden.

"Thanks," I said. "Once the tree is removed Ben can get a team out and do the repairs. My bedroom seems to have survived so I should be able to stay in the house."

"Well, if you find things don't work out then come on over."

Drizzle became a deluge and chased us inside. Felicity helped me tidy the storm's mess whilst we waited for the men to come off the roof. By late afternoon they'd cleared most of the broken branches and debris and stapled heavy-duty plastic sheets across the beams to protect against the elements.

Ben hadn't uttered a word to me since the morning. He gave Felicity and Tom a ride home and returned a while later with a foil wrapped parcel of sandwiches which we devoured in silence. I cleared away and stood at the sink, the sky beyond the window orange and mauve as the sun descended and storm clouds regrouped.

He leaned against the counter. "Are you staying here tonight?"

I faced him. "Of course."

"I can stay over if you want."

I smiled. "No. I'm grateful, but I'll call if there's a problem. Besides, Filly said I can stay at theirs if I need to, but I'd rather not if this is liveable."

"The worst of the storm seems to be over, but you know where to find me."

Yes, I knew. I also knew I had to put space between us. Whatever I thought I felt about him, I couldn't expose myself to more hurt and humiliation, and he had potential for dishing large quantities of both.

I rigged Tom's donated camp light next to my bed and shut the bedroom door to block out the plastic sheeting's crackling.

My mobile phone rang. I prodded the screen and lay back on my pillow.

"How's things?" Shelly sang into my ear.

"With me or the house?"

"I heard. Bad luck, man," she said.

"I'm not used to storms like this. My roof's got a great big hole in it." I lifted the phone away from my ear. Something rattled overhead.

She gave a throaty laugh. "I hope you've got good insurance."

"Once the tree's gone, repairs shouldn't take too long. The damage hasn't extended much further than the roof and a bit of ceiling. Lucky for me the garden wall took the brunt. The roof caught the top branches."

"I'll come around tomorrow night and we can christen the sky bar," she said.

Any excuse for a piss up. "Can I ask you something?" I chewed my lip, nervous my question would stir a hornet's nest.

"Anything. Unless I don't know the answer, of course."

"The thing between Ben and Tracy."

A toilet flushed and a door squeaked.

"Are you on the loo?"

She laughed. "Girl's gotta go. What do you want to know?"

"So, because of the storm and the roof, I stayed over at Ben's last night and found a fingernail under his sofa. Other than you, Tracy's the only one around here with fancy acrylics. I wondered how serious things are, you know, with them."

"Kind of on-off." She hesitated. "Why? Are you interested in him?"

"No. I just wondered at his reaction to me finding the nail."

She sucked in air. "Have you slept with him?"

"No." Semantics.

"Well then, since you're asking my opinion, stay away from him. Tracy is bad news, babe, you do not want to be messing with her business."

The ceiling rattled again. I rolled off the bed and stood with my back against the windowsill. "I will. Thanks. I'll pop around for lunch tomorrow. Will you be on shift?"

"All day, double shift."

I ended the call. The house fell silent, as if holding its breath. The object rolled across the ceiling boards, from the point above the light fitting to the wardrobe. I followed the sound. Gooseflesh rose on my arms as the room's warmth dissipated. I went for the lamp and shone the light into the wardrobe's dark recess. Nothing.

In the hallway, Ben's ladder leaned into the damaged ceiling. Before I could lose my nerve, I darted out of the bedroom with the lamp slung over my wrist and climbed in the void. My breath clouded the frigid air. The roof cavity stank of plastic and damp wood, and the small light did nothing to illuminate the vast darkness.

The roof trusses were rough under my hands and snagged my socks as I felt my way along, stepping on the wood beams, balancing myself so I wouldn't slip and fall through the ceiling boards. In the corner above where I estimated the wardrobe to be, formed by a retaining wall and the outer wall, lay a manila shoebox.

I placed the lamp on a truss and crawled on all fours until I could reach the box. I tucked it up the front of my t-shirt and crawled backwards to the truss and then retraced my steps to the ladder.

In my bedroom, I sat on the bed and lifted the box's lid. A whiff of age and mildew wafted out. I smoothed the duvet and laid out the box's contents. A beige and black polka dot scarf, soft and sheer. One corner had been snagged on something and had a small frayed hole. A photo frame with bevelled glass, ribbon detail and gilt feet, from which a sepia photograph of a baby smiled from the frame's oval window. I adjusted the metal stand and stood the frame on my bedside table.

Beneath a pile of envelopes, secured with faded red string, lay a red and green plaid man's tie, the fabric wrinkled but bright, unmarred by the passage of time. I flicked through the envelopes, each addressed in neat fountain pen script, stamped and postmarked, the top one dated August third, nineteen thirty. Each had a slit across the top, the little fragments of torn paper aged to a golden yellow.

Last, a small rusted tin, Edgeworth Pipe Tobacco emblazoned on the front. I pried open the lid and brushed a thumb across the smooth metal, then dipped a finger into the clutter of treasures within.

"Connie, this is Veronica Rowland." I sat against the bed's base with an arm tucked under my knees. I'd had the best night's sleep in weeks and buzzed with energy.

She sounded less than pleased to hear my voice. "How are you? I heard about the storm damage."

Of course she'd heard. "Do you have any information on the house's history, or at least know where I can find out about the previous owners?"

The line went silent. I could hear the faint clicking of nails on a keyboard.

"Connie?"

"Sorry, I'm going through the sale notes but I can't see anything."

Her linear approach to my question exasperated me. "Is there an archive or library which might have something?"

"I can find out and let you know," she said.

"Right." Motivation and initiative a fat zero. "Thanks." For nothing. I selected Felicity's number from my phone's contacts.

"Veronica. We haven't seen you for days, is everything all right?"

Other than a ghost who insists on calling me by my mother's nickname? And did I mention the surprise box of goodies? "Where can I get info on the house, past owners and stuff?"

"Oh gosh, now you're asking," she said. "You can check with Father Murphy, he's the font of all sacred knowledge around here. Or there's Arthur Mackie. He's about a hundred, he'll know stuff about the mill. I'll ring Elaine and we'll get him round for a cuppa. I could do with a lazy afternoon and some home baking."

And gallons of alcohol. "Fab." I checked the time. "I'll see if I can catch Father Murphy now, before he disappears on a pilgrimage." An unbidden thought of Arthur flashing his neighbours popped into my mind.

CHAPTER 7

FATHER MURPHY STRAIGHTENED from deadheading his Christmas roses and squinted into coruscated sunlight. "Well, hello again," he said. He removed a grubby gardening glove and stepped from beneath the trees, extending a hand for me to shake. "You're the early bird."

"I'm on a mission," I said. "Scrounging for history on my house. I hoped you could help."

"Ah," he said, "I'm taking advantage of this rare spell of sunshine to fix up the disarray after the storm, but I'd be happy to be of assistance." He clutched his gloves and secateurs and rocked on his heels. "You're fortunate that tree didn't do more damage to your roof. I take it you've had young Benjamin up there sorting out the repairs." His eyes, sharp beneath soft grey eyebrows, locked with mine, and I experienced a moment of intense discomfort.

"Tell you what," he said, "I have tea and scones. I

don't have anywhere to be until noon, so if you'd care to join me, we can gain a few pounds and discuss what it is you're after."

I trailed him through the churchyard, pausing at intervals whilst he hauled branches off the path and discussed dandelions, rhododendrons, and the eroded headstones of the long dead. Once at his desk, Father Murphy transformed into a staid cleric. The genial chatterbox slid black-rimmed glasses onto his nose and scanned the bookshelf, a ceiling high monstrosity packed with volumes, ancient and less so, in variations of red, black and brown spines, older ones titled in gold lettering, many obscured by wear.

"These records date back to eighteen thirty-seven," he mumbled. "Baptisms, marriages, burials. There's journals and various miscellanea. If you want to go further back you can get in touch with the county records office, but lots of this stuff's online now." He glanced at me over the top of his glasses, "Roughly when do you want to start searching?"

"Around nineteen hundred," I said. "If I can't find anything useful, I'll go further back."

"Have you asked around, spoken to Arthur Mackie? He's our oldest resident and would know more about the goings on here than what you'll find in parish records."

"Sure," I said. I eyed the volumes with trepidation. Before I could search for information online I'd need names and dates. Searching the church's records would take weeks.

"Once you have a better idea of what you're looking for we can make an appointment for you to come in and view our registers. I might stand corrected, but I recall reading somewhere that the mill belonged to one particular family from around nineteen two to nineteen thirty-two. I can do a bit of digging and see what I come up with."

Felicity gaped. "You want to go through all those records?" She stacked the dinner dishes into the dishwasher whilst Tom poured another round of drinks. He and Filly flopped into a chair together, like a pair of synchronised swimmers diving backwards into a pool.

"What do you hope to find?" Tracy kicked off her shoes and folded her legs beneath her. She leaned her elbow on the sofa's backrest and ran her nails through her hair, tugging and rearranging the dark tufts.

"A bit of history." I held back telling them about the shoebox. "I'll have to source names and dates before I can start looking, but Father Murphy says there's a period up to the nineteen thirties where the mill was owned by the same family."

"Fire destroyed the mill in nineteen thirty-two," Gareth said. He perched on the sofa's arm, a hand on Tracy's shoulder, stroking her neck. "Ben got the commission to rebuild after a businessman invested in developing the property, but then the guy upped sticks after a few months and took off."

"Arthur will answer all your questions," Elaine said. "We're invited to his for coffee next week."

Bill waggled his eyebrows. "Make sure he's wearing his trousers." We all laughed.

"The fire wiped everyone out," Tracy said, shifting her position so Gareth's hand fell away. "Maybe there's nothing to find. What's the point of dredging up the past? The ghost exists in your imagination."

"You're an arse, Tracy," Felicity said. Tom patted her hand and nodded.

Tracy sneered. "I think you'll find Ben would agree with me." She ran her tongue around her lips in a slow circle, eyes on me. Gareth went to perch on a chair near the window, his emotions raw, tangible. Maybe there'd been times in my marriage people had looked at me and thought the same thing.

"Arthur was born round about nineteen twenty," Elaine said. "He knows everything about the parish and I guarantee he'll have all sorts of anecdotes and artefacts. I'll bet the St Agnes Museum can't wait to get hold of his stash of memorabilia."

"Are you looking for anything in particular?" Gareth said.

"I want to know who lived there," I said. "What they did, what happened to them. There's got to be relatives around, someone like Arthur who remembers them."

He sighed, chewed on a thumbnail. "From the minute you moved in there's been one drama or another Ben's had to sort out. People are joking about your ghost and laughing at you. What will it take for you to realise you don't belong."

Swine. "I don't belong? We've already had this conversation. I don't know what your problem is, but I'm going nowhere so maybe you need to get used to the idea?" I was fizzing. "And another thing, Ben's a contractor and gets paid for sorting out my dramas. Don't be fooled into thinking I give a damn what you or anyone else thinks about me."

Gareth's glare turned my insides. Felicity nudged Tom, "Time for a refill, my love." We fell into a silent lull, each of us preoccupied with our own thoughts. I stifled a yawn. Filly caught my eye and twitched a you-can-stay-over-if-you-want eyebrow. Though tempted by the idea of a hot bath, maybe Gareth had a point.

"I'm going to head off," I said. I zipped myself into my coat and felt for the torch buried in my pocket. "Ben's got the electrician coming round first thing." I gave Tracy a look, considered running my tongue around my lips but chickened out. Bitch.

"I thought you'd never come home." Shelly looked a sorry sight huddled on my top step peering out of her hoodie, beanie stretched over her ears. She'd ditched her skirt for a pair of loose-fitting jeans, and swapped heels for UGGs.

"I almost didn't," I said. "Filly offered me to stay over at hers."

"Thanks for not." She took the keys out my hand and unlocked the door. A frosty gust greeted us. "You're welcome." She called into the darkness.

I waved the torch beam around. "Who's welcome?"

"My Nan used to say ghosts don't know they're dead and are friendlier if you welcome them."

"Really?"

"Yep. And I need to be on the good side of this ghost of yours, it's got a scratchy disposition."

No kidding. "Want a cuppa?" She tagged behind with the camp light, our shadows looming above and around us. I ignited the gas cooker and filled a pot of water.

The kitchen door clicked open and Shelly whooped. "Bloody hell, I could have been inside ages ago."

"Ben fixed the damned thing." I kicked the door shut. "I'm going to get a chain fitted, see if my smartarse ghost can undo a chain." Shelly set out the mugs. Twice she shot me a glance and looked away when I caught her eye. "What?"

She scrunched her nose and shrugged. "What, what?"

"Spit it out." Besides being tired, freezing crotchety I'd been so angry and self-absorbed I hadn't thought it odd to find her camped on my doorstep, dressed like a transient.

She clasped her hands and twisted her knuckleduster ring. "I need a place to stay. Temporary. Just for a couple of days. I can help you sort out the roof mess. Anything. I can do anything." Her eyes welled. "Pretty please."

"Of course you can stay," I said. What was I thinking? She'd drive me nuts. Then again, having Shelly as a house guest featured as the least of my worries. "Stay as long as you need."

She flung her arms around me and smothered me in hair. "Thank you."

I extracted myself from her grip, made the tea, and we settled on the sofa. For the first time since we'd met, I faced the real Shelly, miserable and scruffy, her big hair and petite frame doing little to camouflage the obvious. "What's happened? Have you fell out with Dan?"

She dodged my question. "You're not like everyone else I know," she said. She twisted a strand of hair around her finger. "You're young to be married, and divorced, but you've got your shit together and you're a nice person."

I sipped my tea. I wasn't going to let her make this about me.

She plucked at her hair ends. "When I was thirteen I fell in love with a boy in my year. To me, we felt right, you know, special. I confided in a friend about my feelings, someone I trusted. Well, they told everyone, and I got the shit beat out of me by the love of my life. I'd betrayed him by telling our secret. He broke my heart." A tear slid down her cheek. "So, I had nothing to lose and from that day on Sean became Shelly and I dressed and behaved like I wanted to." She burrowed into the cushions. "Found myself frogmarched in to counselling."

When things started going wrong in my marriage, my mother had colluded with Graeme to get me to marriage counselling, then he and the counsellor had minimised my existence, made me the bad guy. I'd arrived at each session physically sick, and left the sessions bruised and a little more damaged. I couldn't imagine what Shelly must have felt.

"Then a month before I turned fifteen my dad moved out." She lay back, swiped at tears. "I hooked up with Daniel at university. He's an amazing guy and we love each other, but he can't handle the reality of things. He supports me and comes with me to appointments at the Tavistock, but he can't deal with what I still have to go through with surgery. Like everyone, he doesn't understand why this is important to me."

"Why did you move here?" I said.

"I had nowhere else to go after university. My mother relocated to Blackpool with her boyfriend, and he has a problem with 'people like me'." She made a one-fingered air quote. "So I decided to give my dad a second chance."

She'd brought no bag or change of clothes. She lived in a bedsit a few doors along from the pub but hadn't hinted of a problem. Whoever her dad was, I'd never seen him and she'd never spoken of him.

I needed sleep and Shelly looked prepared for an

all-nighter. "You can sleep on the futon in my office," I said, "though I can't offer you a hot shower until the electrician's been." I gave her little opportunity to protest, supplied her with pyjamas and bedding and an extra thick blanket, and went to bed.

I tossed and turned, cold and peeved at everyone. I might as well have sat drinking tea with Shelly all night. I hadn't got to the bottom of her dilemma after all and contemplated the risk of letting her move in. There hadn't been anyone for me when I needed help. I'd had to mop up my own tears and find my own way. I'd had no one to run to then, and I didn't have the heart to turn my back on her now.

CHAPTER 8

DENSE FOG SHROUDED THE WOODS and diminished all sound, a disconsolate void in a dystopian landscape. The tree loomed ominous, scraggy branches cluttered with stiff faded rags. In all directions shadowed hulks crouched beyond the diaphanous veil.

Above the fog, the sky lightened to a gloomy blue-grey. Frost crunched beneath my shoes as I crossed the road to view the woods from a different perspective. A couple of miles around the bend to my left lay the church, the pub, and the junction which would take me home. I faced right. A road to and from nowhere. Or somewhere? The night I'd first encountered the tree, Ben said he'd been on his way home from the pub.

The morning we'd walked back the long way around realisation dawned on me and I'd taken a drive to see what secrets lurked beyond our hamlet. Not a hell of a lot existed at all beside a nature reserve and a fork in the road which led onward to a holiday cottage and a farm with a B&B, and if one had a wondering spirit, a further twelve miles of farmland between us and Truro.

Why had he lied?

My fingers ached inside my gloves. I'd left Shelly sleeping and had to get back for Ben and the electrician. I begrudged relinquishing my Saturday freedom, slouching around in my PJs all day if the mood took me. The life I'd created for myself teetered on shaky foundations.

Ben didn't stay after brief introductions. He left the electrician to work his magic, and by 11 we had power. The electrician beat a hasty retreat and Shelly made us a pancake and coffee brunch. She remained lashes and lip gloss free, had slept off her puffy eyes, and buzzed with energy.

"I'm going to straighten up and grab a shower whilst you do the dishes," I said. She trailed me upstairs and flopped onto my bed.

"Let me help you tidy. Dishes can wait." She rolled off the opposite side and lifted the duvet's corners, and kicked my shoebox of treasures which lay half concealed beneath the bed, sans lid. "What's this?" She crouched and lifted the box onto the bed.

"Nothing." My finger hooked into a corner but she held fast and the box ripped. "Damnit Shelly, can you leave my stuff alone?"

If looks could kill. She flounced out the room and a

moment later my office door slammed. I placed the lid on to hold the box together and slid it onto a shelf in my wardrobe. When I emerged from the bathroom half an hour later she sat on my bed holding the photo frame. "Sorry I snapped at you," I said. "I'm not used to sharing my space."

She shrugged. "S'kay. Who's this?"

"Don't know." And a bit of privacy would be grand. "Give me a minute to get dressed and I'll tell you over a cuppa."

When I got downstairs, Shelly sprawled on the sofa sporting pink socks, one with a hole above the big toe. Seven envelopes lay spread across the coffee table, six addressed and postmarked, one with no stamp.

"These four were written by the same person," I said. Childlike handwriting spelt out "Miss Dorothy Killigrew, c/o The Mill, Fallow, Cornwall." The others were addressed in an elaborate cursive hand. I arranged them in date order, placing the unstamped one last in line.

Shelly unfolded the first one, the paper yellowed and lined, the margin rough, torn from a notebook.

25 December 1929

My dearest Dotty

My heart is aching for you. This is truly the worst Christmas day ever. I wish we could be together. Instead,

I am surrounded by noisy chaps creating distraction with their tiresome games. We're confined to barracks so the mess can be prepared for our dinner, and there's rumour we have some sort of entertainment.

I cherish the memory of our last day together, precious Dotty, though I fear your father would have thrashed us senseless had he caught me in your bedroom. (Though well worth the risk, I say!)

I can't wait for the New Year. I shall think of you at midnight. I hope you will be thinking of me.

Please write soon with news of home.

I am most affectionately yours.

Vincent xxx

Shelly waggled her eyebrows. I reached for the letter. "Wait, there's a postscript." Shelly read on: "P.S. I hope you like the scarf. When you wear it, you can think of my touch upon your neck." She stuck out her tongue and feigned nausea.

I laughed. "You've made that up." She folded the note into its envelope.

A knock rattled the door. The smell of damp earth wafted through, followed by Ben. He grinned at me and frowned at Shelly. "What's up?"

"Coffee?"

"Love one." He dropped into a chair and pointed to the envelopes. "What's this?"

"Letters I found in a shoebox in the ceiling." I expected at least a cocked eyebrow, or a sign of interest, but received neither. Instead, he studied the envelopes and lifted the one without the postmark as if contemplating its weight.

"I doubt it. I restored the mill from a ruin," he said, without looking up. "There was no ceiling, no roof, just charred walls and holes where doors and windows used to be. The place burnt to the ground."

Shelly sat to attention, her eyes like saucers.

I stopped at the foot of the stairs as a heaviness settled on my chest. He'd called me a liar. I gripped the banister. I wanted to speak but fury and confusion prevented sensible words from forming.

Rain drops needled the windows. A whiff of overheated wiring drifted down the stairs. The chandelier flickered and the electricity tripped. Shelly yelped, and Ben leapt off the chair and headed across to me. He froze before he reached me, focused on something over my shoulder. "Come here, Vee," he said, reaching a hand towards me.

I didn't want his hand. I wanted to hate him. I seethed.

"Take my hand, now, we need to get out of here."

The air around us cooled. Static crackled and my neck hairs bristled. I took his hand and followed him without a backward glance. Shelly gathered the letters and handed me my keys. Ben jostled us outside into pelting rain and shut the door. We clamoured into his van and he leaned on the steering wheel, his breath ragged, like he'd run a mile instead of a few feet. The house loomed, a shadowed silhouette against a fierce sky.

"What was that all about?" Shelly said, indignant at her wet socks and cold feet.

I wasn't sure I wanted to hear the answer.

Ben reversed onto the road. Tyres skidded in the mud before connecting with the tarmac. He didn't look back at the house, but I could see his eyes fixed on the side mirror, not looking away until we'd reached the junction.

We pulled up outside the bedsit and Shelly's hand curled around my wrist. "I'm staying with Veronica," she said.

"Not today, sweet cheeks."

His tone rankled me. "I invited her to stay."

"Not today. Get out."

"Ben?"

Before I could argue her case, Shelly bolted. I spun in the seat and punched his arm. "How dare you speak to her like that? She is staying at mine." I chased after her and caught hold of her arm. "Ignore him. You're staying with me."

"He hates me. Everyone hates me."

"Nobody hates you. Get in, we'll talk later."

We returned to the van sopping. Ben snapped the shift into gear and pulled away. "Big mistake. You're looking for trouble with this one."

"Shelly. Her name is Shelly."

"Whatever."

Shelly leaned into me. An overwhelming sense of powerlessness swamped me. I wasn't the girl who won arguments. Tears stung and a familiar ache burned in my chest, anger fuelled by humiliation. Who was I fooling with my big life adventure? Deep down, the insignificant girl whose opinions didn't matter cowered. "Drop us back at my house."

Ben shot me a look. "Not a hope in hell of that happening."

Minutes later we stood shivering in his entrance hall. I left my shoes at the door and Shelly peeled off her socks and stood in a puddle. He got us towels and we used his bedroom to change into a selection of his sweatpants and t-shirts.

"Do you mind if I stay here?" Shelly sat on the bed and gathered a cover over her legs.

She shivered, her face pale and drawn. Getting to the bottom of whatever troubled her would have to wait, and Ben's attitude did little to help matters. I didn't need him or his bullshit. "I'll be downstairs. If you need me, call."

"Thanks." She slid beneath the cover and turned to face the window.

Ben sat on the lounge floor facing the fire, the envelopes arranged on the rug.

"What happened at the house?" I said. I contemplated the sofa, but suffered a nailgate flashback and imagined him and Tracy cavorting on the cushions. I lowered myself to the floor and leaned against an easy chair.

"Sometimes you have to walk away from that place, give it space. When it spikes and you hang around, that's when things get nasty."

"What spikes? What gets nasty?"

He hugged his knees, inhaled and held his breath for several heartbeats. "When I worked on the house a lot of weird stuff went on. At first, I thought I was imagining things, but sometimes things got a bit frightening. I told Filly, and on bad days she'd either sit with me or we'd abandon site. On good days I tolerated it. Ended up I had to bring in labourers from further afield or do the work myself because I couldn't get anyone local to work with me."

"Filly knew about this and didn't say anything to me."

Ben ran his fingers through his hair. "Don't blame her. I told her not to say anything."

"Thanks a lot, that's bloody great. Good to know my friends are looking out for me. But then I'm not really a friend, am I? Just an outsider. Do you all get together at Filly's to discuss the latest spike in my house?"

"It's not like that, Vee. We didn't know what to say without sounding nuts. We agreed to wait and see. Maybe we were wrong and the house would settle. The place reacts to moods and I'm sorry to say, but you're a catalyst."

"I'm a catalyst?"

"Filly says you're passionate. So yeah, moody." He

pressed his fingers into his eye sockets. "This is coming out wrong."

"Moody. Passionate. A catalyst? Gareth's adamant I'm an outsider who doesn't belong. So what, this is all my fault?"

"Gareth's got a beef with the mill in general. He's not alone. There's a few around here who didn't want the rebuild. I made a lot of people angry when I took the job."

"And the shoebox. You think I'm lying."

He leaned forward and touched my knee. "I didn't say you're lying. More like someone's pranking you." He twitched his head and rolled his eyes upward.

"Oh, you think Shelly put the box there. What, she snuck into the house and climbed into the roof without me noticing?"

"Do you have a better explanation?"

Of course not. "I'll find out the truth. Then I'll decide how to deal with things." I'd invested my entire divorce settlement into the house and damn well intended to stick around.

Chapter 9

High winds, incessant rain and the twilight gloom reminded me why I loathed winter. Ben and I migrated to his kitchen for a coffee and sat at the window in awkward silence. Sure, I had questions about what he'd experienced in my house, but I needed to understand why he and Felicity had chosen to hide the details from me.

As I formulated my question, Tracy's car pulled in the drive and parked beside the van. Ben cursed and gave me an indiscernible look as he went for the door. She entered the hallway and her arms snaked about his waist, mouth aimed for his. He grasped her wrists and muttered something inaudible.

"Veronica?" She wrenched herself from his grip and strutted into the kitchen, her body rigid, hands on hips. Her eyes were dark and void of warmth. "You get around, don't you?"

Embarrassment percolated through me like hot wax. "Yeah, I suppose I do," I said, my tone tart. "And so do you by the looks of things. How's Gareth?" I'd had my share of in-the-face glares, veiled threats and rival antagonism, but then I'd been the wife, the one who had the man, the one with all the power. Here, I was nobody, an outsider to this insidious group of people. I glared back.

She poked a nail into my chest. "Don't fuck with me, girlie."

Ben drew her away. He towed her to the door, exerting such force the wood smacked against the wall as he tugged her behind him to the car. I couldn't hear what they said over the thrum of blood rushing in my ears, but the waspish look on Tracy's face reflected pure hatred.

They argued, and I wanted to be as far away from them as possible. I went for my shoes, squeezed my feet into the wet leather, and took the envelopes. Ben's garden gate opened onto a bridle path which ran behind his house, perfect for an impromptu escape.

At the junction, I realised my house keys were in the van. I'd also abandoned Shelly. I wrestled my conscience and decided I'd sooner freeze to death on my front step than go back. I shouldered through the side gate to my backyard and for once appreciated my open back door.

My heart fluttered as I stepped into the kitchen, an intruder in my own home. I flipped the light switch on and felt the radiator. So far so good. I made a circuit of downstairs. Upstairs, the roof plastic crackled. My heart pulsed in my throat. I went up, one step at a time. No atmosphere. No fire and brimstone. I thought about the letters, about Dorothy Killigrew and Vincent. I thought about Shelly, and about the shoebox.

My phone vibrated. Excellent timing, as always. "Hey mum." I sat on the top step.

"Four weeks to Christmas, darling, and still no invitation to your housewarming."

"I know, I've been busy," I said. "I'm almost settled then we'll see, okay?"

Long sigh. "You're being tedious, Roo. What game are you playing?"

"Roo . . ."

I shot to my feet. "I'll phone you back." I ended the call, pocketed my phone, and descended to the middle landing, heart hammering, back pressed to the wall. No sudden temperature drop or lightshow, no icy breath or spectral caress, but a smell, acrid, sweet and nauseating, tinged with the sulphuric odour of burnt hair.

Oh God.

The doorknocker's staccato clacks struck me like a cattle prodder. I flung myself down the remaining stairs and wrenched the door open.

My keys dangled from Ben's finger. Behind him, Shelly stood, shoeless, arms folded across her chest, mouth puckered in a sulk. I let them in, took my keys, and dropped them in a bowl on the bookshelf.

Ben slipped his hands into his pockets and faced me,

eyebrows raised in wary deference. "How did you get in?"

"Care of you-know-who. Back door."

He fiddled with his loose change. His eyes held mine. "I'm sorry for involving you in something that's not your business."

What could I say? "Wrong place, wrong time."

"I'm going to my room." Shelly elbowed me aside and took off up the stairs. Her footsteps thumped across the ceiling and a door banged.

"You can't be serious about him moving in?"

I ingurgitated the lingering pall of charred flesh, and shouted. "Don't assume since you've assigned yourself knight in shining armour, or because you've slept in my bed, that you know me or have the right to question my actions."

He took a step back and raised his hands in submission. "Sorry. I just mean you need to know what you're dealing with. Don't let that vulnerable damsel-in-despair look fool you."

I ignored his snipe at her. What I did in my house had nothing to do with anyone. We scowled at one another until he broke the deadlock. "Can I explain, about Tracy?"

"If you feel you must."

"We had a thing," he said. "I'm not proud of myself because Gareth's a decent guy. She's just . . . tenacious, goes for what she wants." He paused, his discomfort plain to see. "And always gets what she's after, one way or another. When things don't go her way she makes them, if you know what I mean."

Oh, I knew what he meant. All the same, I had no idea why he felt the need to explain, considering his relationship wasn't my business. "Does Filly know?"

"She knows but doesn't say anything. She knows what Tracy's like."

Seemed to me Felicity didn't like saying a whole hell of a lot to anyone about anything. A regular fence dweller.

"Tracy hasn't always been like this. She used to be cool, and funny. She and Gareth were happy together. Then one day, out the blue, she came on to me. I was engaged at the time," he said. The coins in his pocket clinked as he fidgeted.

Engaged. Shit. I needed a drink. He followed me to the kitchen and leaned against the worktop. I took two bottles of beer from the fridge, popped the lids, and handed him one.

"I was having a rough time, and this place got to me." He waved a hand through the air. "Cost me my relationship. I had nothing left to lose, you know how these things go."

Nope, no idea. How I saw things, he cost himself his own relationship. Petitioning sympathy from me was like quelling a fire with a colander.

"When you moved in things changed," he said. "For the first time in a long time I felt like there was light at the end of a very long, dark tunnel. On the day of the storm, I broke things off with her. She went mad and laid into me, that's how her fingernail got under the couch."

I studied his profile as he picked at the bottle's label, sensuous lips pressed in a firm unforgiving line. My legs trembled, like I'd been carrying a load and someone lifted the burden. I wanted to laugh, or cry, or scream, but couldn't decide the dominant sensation, or where the emotions came from.

A metallic object clinked as it rolled down the stairs and spun across the floor. Ben reached the thing first, a simple gold signet ring engraved with the letters G.H., and slid it onto his pinkie finger.

"The ring's from the shoebox," I said. I called up. "Shelly, are you all right?"

Rain tapped against the plastic sheeting. Ben slid an arm around me. I could feel his pulse. Or perhaps my own. "Do you want to go check on him?"

"Her. I'm going to check on her."

He expelled a breath. "I think you know who the culprit is in all this crap. Who do you think rolled the ring down the stairs?"

The bathroom window's faint glow cast scant light. Shelly's door remained shut. The envelopes lay in a neat arrangement on my bed. Ben glanced at me and cocked an eyebrow. "Did you do that?"

I shook my head.

"See what I mean? Where's the box?"

"In my wardrobe."

He retrieved the shoebox and sat on the bed, fished

out the tobacco tin, snapped open the lid and upended the contents. Little tufts of dust, a folded and yellowed newspaper cutting, and an eclectic assortment of items dropped onto the cover.

I turned on the lamp and pointed. "There's that too."

He lifted the photo frame off my bedside table and ran his thumb along the bevelled edge. "Babies all look the same to me. This one looks like my sister Colette's little girl, Penny, at the same age, same dark curls." He replaced the frame, removed the ring, and dropped it into the pile of treasures.

Wind plucked at the plastic and a mournful wail swept over the roof's jagged edges. I looped a finger through the ring and the light glinted off the gold. "Some of these letters to Dorothy are signed by a Gladys Hendry."

Ben glanced at the envelopes. "GH. But it's a man's ring."

"Her husband's maybe?"

"Are there any other GH initials on your research list?"

"No. Just Gladys Hendry's. That reminds me, Father Murphy called yesterday. He went through some old boundary maps and records stored in the church's strong box and said the Bassett family owned the mill for several generations before selling to the Killigrews in nineteen hundred and one. With a bit of luck Arthur will know more about them."

Ben scratched his head. "I'll ask around, see if anyone

knows about the Hendry link." He gathered the items and funnelled them into the tin, repacked the box and dusted the cover. "If we can find out who owns this box we might find our answer."

I plucked the letter out of the unstamped envelope. The paper felt rough and rumpled, as if scrunched and then pressed flat to iron out the creases. Dried ghost tears dotted the page where the ink had run.

29 Augu-- 1930

Mrs Gladys Hen-ry

Despite your efforts to have my baby taken fro- me before I could see her, the midwife show-- me a kindness and let me hold her f-- a moment as they cut the cord. I have named her A----- ---ch --- the name Vincent chose for her, named after h-- grandmother.

You have taken everything from me. You have br--ken my h-----. Will she know me? Will --- --- w--- a wonderful person her father was?

I can n---- forgive you for what you have done to us. The hatr--- I f--- for you burns my soul.

I beg you, take good care of our daug----.
D----thy

Ben leaped off the bed at the first bang. Two more reverberated through the house. An icy gust of air snatched the letter from my grip, a misshapen paper aeroplane which fluttered across the room and clung to the window pane. Around the edges, invisible breath formed fine condensation.

I reached the window and peeled the paper away. My strange man stood by the gate posts and looked at me from shadowed eyes beneath a floppy fringe.

Come.

I jumped at Ben's touch. I held the man's gaze, afraid to lose him to the twilight. "Do you see him?" I whispered. The man clutched his boater to his chest and stared at us.

Ben leaned forward and looked out. "See who?"

CHAPTER 10

COME.

I turned away from the window and ran down the stairs. A cold gust drew me to the kitchen, and outside, the man waited on the path beyond the ruin.

"Where are you going?" Ben caught my wrist. "It's freezing out."

"Follow him." I twisted out of his hold and ran after the man as he flickered between the trees. When I reached the rag tree I bent, hands on my thighs, and sucked in mouthfuls of air to ease the stitch in my side. Ben came up behind me, out of breath. The man beckoned from beneath the tree's dripping branches. "Do you see him?"

"There's nothing here, Vee."

I gestured with both hands. "It's the man I told you about, the one I followed the night you found me here. He wants us to look at something in the tree."

Ben squelched through mud and slid across slimy wet roots. "Tell me when I'm near him."

"Be careful. He's right by you."

He leaned against the tree's trunk and for a moment their forms merged, the man's radiance enveloping Ben in an iridescent glow. He hunched his shoulders and his breath plumed. "Can you still see him?"

When he stepped back, the shimmering light faded and we were alone. Dregs of rag and ribbon dripped on us, and each gust of wind caused a shower. "He's gone," I said. "I can't believe you didn't see him, see his light."

"You should have put a jacket on, you're shivering." Ben found his way back to me and wrapped his arms around me. He made a quick assessment of the vicinity. "What's he look like?"

The question wasn't what he looked like, rather who. "Let's go." The tree gave me the horrors. Water dripped on me like remnant tears and sadness contaminated my skin. I extracted myself from his warmth and negotiated the mass of roots, thankful the gloom masked my disappointment.

At the top of the path, flames flickered between the branches. Ben reached my side and gasped. "What the hell?"

My bewildered mind struggled to make sense of what I saw. "Fire?" Realisation struck me like an electric charge. "Jesus, Shelly."

We ran. Fire sensors squealed. Ben sprinted up the

stairs, flung my office door wide and strode towards the blaze. The fire consumed the curtains and blistered the paint on the walls and ceiling. Bits of flaming fabric dropped on the carpet and ignited small pinprick fires. He slid his sleeves over his hands and twisted the window latch, tore the curtains from the railing, and bundled them out of the window.

The carpet fires died, trampled beneath his boots. Acrid smoke swirled around us. Soot marred the walls and haloed the ceiling, and the curtain rail hung lopsided, its screws wrenched from the wall. He ran a forearm across his forehead and wiped his hands on his jeans.

Adrenaline sizzled in my veins. My stomach cramped. "Where is she?" Crumpled bedding and a pillow full of blotched mascara, clothes and shoes were scattered across the floor, no Shelly.

Ben's lips formed inaudible words. Panic roared in my ears. He shook me, and almost unhinged my shoulders from their sockets. "He's in the bathroom."

My senses slotted into place and my eyes settled on a candle holder on the windowsill. Shelly appeared in the doorway wrapped in a towel. The penny didn't drop. Instead, she looked from the window to Ben to me and wrinkled her nose. "What's going on?"

I snapped. "Can't you hear the alarm? You almost burnt my fucking house down."

"Whoa, don't shout at me. I didn't do it." She took a couple of steps towards me and changed her mind. "Why would I burn the house with me in it?"

She had a point. "You left the candle burning."

"No, no. No candle." She sidestepped Ben and his clenched fists and prodded the candle holder. "Look, no candle." She turned tear-filled eyes on me. "I've done some sketchy shit in my life, but I would never do anything like this."

The contempt on Ben's face curdled my blood. I touched his arm and flinched when he turned on me. "Don't say I didn't warn you, Veronica. This..." He stabbed a finger at the window and then at Shelly, "isn't the half of it."

Shelly adjusted the towel and hovered, unsure of her next move.

"Get dressed," I said. "I'll make the front room up for you." To Ben, "How do I turn off this racket?"

A young girl in school uniform stood on my front step. She had the same elfin look as Felicity, but with long dark hair and grape-green eyes. Her freckled face crinkled into a smile which I couldn't help returning. In her arms she cradled an ancient hat box which she handed to me. "Hi, I'm Penny. Aunt Filly's niece. Mum said to bring you this."

Once inside, she fluttered around. Words tumbled over one another as she examined my books and ornaments, and peered at a small painting propped on the bookshelf. "Where'd you get this?"

"It's a graduation gift from my father."

She pursed her lips and nodded in an adult fashion. She poked her head into the kitchen, and walked around the dining table, assessing its peculiar shape. Her eyes swivelled upward. "Can I go up?"

She'd inherited more than Filly's looks. "Sure." I placed the hat box on a chair, lifted the lid and picked out a pack of envelopes tied with a faded ribbon, and lay them on the coffee table. I unfolded a christening robe, handmade and embellished with lace hems and cuffs embroidered with miniature flowers, and a small crocheted blanket, each folded in tissue paper, dappled from age. On the bottom lay three photo frames.

The ceiling creaked as Penny navigated the rooms. I sat and balanced two brass frames on my knees and held a black enamel one which displayed a sepia print of a familiar boy with a mischievous grin, fringe flopped across his forehead. My heart pounded.

One brass frame held a photograph of a young girl, fair hair tied in plaits, chin pressed into her shoulder as she waved to the camera. The second image showed a seated woman, maybe in her twenties, the same shy look and fair hair, demure, hands folded in her lap, the hint of a smile on her lips.

"There's a guy in the backyard, Veronica." Penny called from the house's depths.

A chill prickled up my spine. I placed the frames on

the sofa and met her bouncing down the stairs. We stood at the back door looking into the empty garden.

"He was here a minute ago, I swear," Penny said. She stepped outside and pointed to the spot where the path cut into the woods. "You need to watch out for weirdos, they come to see the rag tree and wander around like they own the place. They think it's magic or holy or something. Father Murphy catches a hissy when they go to the church to ask about it." She spun on her heel, the man forgotten, and ran back upstairs.

I had no reference point when it came to children, but I knew quiet was bad, and something held her enthralled. I made myself a coffee and tore open a box of ice lollies and called her. She sprawled on the sofa and dissected her lolly in colour order. "Do you have kids?"

"No."

"Who's the baby in the photo next to your bed?"

"I don't know. I found it in a box similar to yours," I said.

"Where's your husband?"

I eyed her over the mug's rim. "Who says I'm married?"

"You have rings. Why do you live with a boy who dresses like a girl?"

"You ask a lot of questions."

"My granny says an enquiring mind leaves no stone unturned."

Granny sounded as misguided as my mother. "Is that

so?"

"Who started the fire?"

"It was an accident."

"Who's Ruth?"

Shit. My hand trembled as I drained my coffee dregs. "None of your business."

She licked each side of her lolly stick and rapped a beat on her thumbnail, matching the rhythm with intermittent foot taps. She glanced at me and narrowed her eyes. I recognised her tactic. Bloody sociopath. "Where do you live, Penny?"

"Near the cider farm."

"How did you get here?"

"I told you. Mum's visiting Aunt Filly."

Shelly's unexpected explosion through the front door interrupted my rebound interrogation and heralded Penny's hasty departure. As she left, Penny gave Shelly the once over and mumbled under her breath.

Shelly pulled a tongue at her. "What's up, Babe?" She removed her jacket and sat, knees apart, and gave me an eyeful of underwear beneath her skirt. "I'm on my break and I'm starving."

"Penny brought more stuff around." I indicated the hat box. She's had a good nose around too so don't be surprised if your stuff's been gone through."

She grinned. "She's a pain in the ass, that one. What smells so good?"

"Casserole in the slow cooker. Ben's coming for

dinner. I can make you a sandwich."

"Got any shots?" She sprang off the sofa and raided the kitchen cupboards whilst I opened a can of tuna.

"Have a beer, there's a couple of cold ones in the fridge."

"No, I'll bloat. Where's the Absinthe?" Her physique guaranteed she'd never bloat. Like, ever. Not even if she drowned in a beer vat. "I need a stiffy." She poured a shot of whisky into a coffee mug, knocked it back, and made a face. "Ugh, you need to get a better selection of booze in this crib."

"I had a good selection a week ago."

She cackled. "Gimme that." She devoured her sandwich, checked her reflection in the window and blew me a kiss. "Don't wait up."

By seven, I had the food ready and the table set. I considered candles, then remembered I'd trashed them all after Shelly's mishap. I did my hundredth loop around the room. What would we talk about? I had no idea why I had the jitters. We weren't strangers, after all.

I showered, retrieved my hairdryer from Shelly's room, and gave my hair a blast. I slipped my dress's soft folds over my head and stood at the mirror. I examined myself from every visible angle, adjusted my boobs and patted my hips. I applied lip balm and puckered my lips.

Whenever my mother had caught me titivating, she'd say, 'Roo, you can't fix ugly'. I smoothed the fabric, brushed my hair and slipped on a pair of sandals.

I did a quick tidy, sprayed fragrance on my bedding, and swallowed a wave of anxiety and nausea. What the hell was I doing?

As I passed through the bedroom doorway, I flicked the light switch and darkness engulfed me. No light emanated from downstairs. The air cooled. I fumbled for the switch but the light didn't respond.

I had no focal point in the pitch black. I clutched the doorframe. My breath laboured. Feather light fingers touched my elbow. Another frigid set of fingers crept up the back of my neck, slid into my hair, and tightened their grip until my head wrenched backward.

"Roo . . ."

A phantasmal voice snarled.

Then screams. Long wavering high-pitched banshee wails, trilling shrieks, and mournful howls.

Nefarious hands shoved me.

I toppled and fell. My knees and hands broke my fall and I crawled across the hallway until I touched tile and got my bearings. I shoved the bathroom door shut, twisted the lock and shrunk into a corner.

Warm liquid soaked my dress and spread across the tiles beneath me.

CHAPTER 11

BEN'S CASUAL POISE GROUNDED ME as I dished out our meal, desperate to keep moving in case my knees gave way and I collapsed. He poured our drinks, and at the table took the chair facing the stairs, which left me with my back exposed to unimaginable horrors lurking above.

"Are you sure you're all right? You're jittery as hell."

I feigned a smile and clinked our glasses. "Cheers. I'm fine. Nothing major. I don't mean to be distracted."

"I spoke with Colette earlier," he said. "She said she sent you an old box of things, more letters. Apparently Penny hasn't stopped talking about her visit. Seems you made an impression."

No kidding. "She could see the man from the tree," I said, "in broad daylight."

His fork stalled halfway to his mouth. "Are you sure it was him?"

"Pretty sure. Who else would it be?"

The dimple at the corner of his lip twitched. "Do you think she realised he's a ghost?"

"She thought he was a tourist who'd come to see the tree." I gestured to the boxes I'd left on the Papasan chair. "I'm going to go through the letters, see if there's any familiar names or anyone else I can research. Do you know where Colette got the box?"

He shrugged. "No, I didn't think to ask. I'll give you a hand with the letters."

We ate, and made plans to complete my roof repairs and tidy the fire damage. All the while I fixated on micro sounds emanating from upstairs.

Ben slid his chair back and stood. "I'll help clear away and we can make a start."

"On what?"

His eyebrows knit together. "The letters."

"I thought you were just being polite."

He balanced our glasses on the stacked plates and called over his shoulder. "Another drink?" He returned from the kitchen with a bottle of beer and a glass of wine for me. "What's with the photo?"

I turned in my chair and followed his gaze. The photo frame from my bedside table stood on the mid landing. My stomach knotted. "Just before you arrived things went a bit weird." A tremor spread through my body and infected my voice. "Scary weird."

He touched my shoulder. "Do you want to go for a

walk? Get some fresh air?"

I laughed. The kind of unhinged outburst that got people sectioned. "I could walk all the way to Truro for fresh air and still have to come back." I gulped a mouthful of wine, set my glass down and stood on unsteady legs. He gathered me in his arms and held me. I breathed his scent and looped my arms around him, safe, even if for a moment.

We cleared the table and I stacked the dishwasher whilst he unpacked the hatbox. I snatched the frame off the landing and placed it face down on the coffee table.

Ben studied the three photos from Colette's box. "And you're sure this is the man you saw at the tree?"

"I'm certain. He bears a remarkable resemblance to you. Maybe a relative?"

He snorted. "Who knows? We're all related in some way around here."

"If everyone's lived here forever someone must know something," I said. "I get the feeling I'm being kept in the dark about things." I sorted the two packs of envelopes into date order to create a rough timeline from December nineteen twenty-nine to August nineteen thirty.

First, Vincent's Christmas letter to Dorothy. Then, on January fifteenth he wrote to say he'd be home on leave in February. His words dashed around the page, written in haste. He told Dorothy they would be a perfect family, and he intended to ask her father for his blessing. "Dorothy must have written to Vincent between Christmas and

January fifteenth with news of her pregnancy."

"There's nothing for around then," Ben said.

"Then Vincent wrote on January twenty-second saying he'd be home February third. And wrote again on January twenty-ninth saying he'd save up to buy her an engagement ring." He'd used every bit of paper to express his delight, and love. I rotated the page and followed his words around the edges, arrows which pointed overleaf, asterisks and underlines, and lots of kisses. "The next one is dated February twentieth."

"Here's an earlier one, February fifteenth." He offered the letter.

"Dorothy wrote to Mrs Hendry asking to see her. She's told her she's expecting a baby, conceived the day before Vincent left for duty. Which explains the one of February twentieth where Gladys Hendry's refused to see Dorothy."

Ben frowned as he read Gladys's letter, "I enclose five pounds and trust this will provide sufficiently for you in the interim. I will be in contact with Mrs Killigrew in due course to discuss your circumstance." He elbowed me. "Nice. I wish a fiver could provide sufficiently for me."

"You and me both. It might have been a lot of money back then."

Ben waved another letter. "June thirteenth, Dorothy to Gladys. She's been to the clinic and the baby is faring well. She begs forgiveness . . . something lying heavy on her heart."

I took the letter and read. "The week after Vincent's funeral I saw you put his tie in the tree. I took it. I couldn't bear to think of anything of Vincent's being out there in the dark and cold." I checked the date. "Pass me the letter of June nineteenth."

He handed me the letter and huddled beside me. We read together.

19th June 1930
Dorothy,

I noticed a wildflower posy on Vincent's grave today. I imagine you're the culprit?

Your admission that you removed my son's tie from the tree is appalling, to say the least. How dare you? That tie is the one he wore on the day of his accident. You have no right to desecrate his memory.

Surely you understand the vicar would not appreciate that I have visited the tree, regardless of the purpose. To his mind the tree is pagan, not worthy of God-fearing Christians, nor the memory of our son. My presence at the tree was private and personal and of no business of yours to repeat.

Please confirm the expected date of your confinement. I have contacted Mrs Killigrew to discuss the matter of adoption.

Sincerely,
Mrs G. Hendry

I folded the letter and reached for the shoebox. "Vincent's tie," I said. The tie appeared pristine. Nothing to suggest its fate. Sight of the thing made me queasy.

"She'd have been six months gone in June, assuming Vincent left in December, so her baby would have been due in September."

"No, August." I unfolded Dorothy's tearstained letter of August twenty-ninth. "Gladys took her baby away from her, broke the poor girl's heart. Vincent wanted their baby named after his grandmother."

"This is the last one." He gave me the envelope with Dorothy's scrawl on it.

I read the letter and checked the envelope. "Where's the date?"

"No date."

"Dear Mrs Hendry. I would be grateful if you could come to the mill for tea. I will be leaving soon and wish to resolve our differences. Dorothy." I chewed my lip. "Dorothy left. She moved away."

"What are you thinking?" Ben leaned back, hands behind his head, put his feet on the coffee table and crossed his ankles.

"How old would their daughter be now?"

Ben worked a calculation on his fingers. "She'd be late eighties."

I sprang off the sofa and walked a circuit around the room. "We need to find her, and find out where Dorothy went."

Ben looked perplexed. "To what end?"

"She deserves to know what happened to her mother." I poked the air. "And to him. Tree man. He's Vincent. They're her parents."

He laughed. "You don't know that. Besides, if she's still alive she probably knows all this."

I lifted the photo frame. "Look at him. This is Vincent. I'm sure of it. This is who I see. This is the guy." I flicked an anxious glance at the stairs.

"Then she could be their daughter." He flipped the frame and we stared at the baby. "And this?" He pointed to the other brass frames. "Dorothy?"

Dorothy Killigrew. "I'll get my laptop. Let's see if we can trace her."

Ben got to his feet. "I'll make us a coffee. When are you seeing Arthur?"

I gripped the stair rail. "We were meant to see him a couple of weeks ago, but Elaine said he's been in hospital. I'll check with her tomorrow, see if he's any better."

I reached the top landing and stood rooted to the spot, hands clammy, heart racing. Ben's presence offered slight comfort. I whispered, self-conscious, but driven by desperation. "I'm going to figure this out Vincent, I promise you."

A bolt of static energy struck me. I lost my footing and dropped to the floor. In my ear, grinding, like teeth gritted in rage. I clung to the banister and curled myself into a ball as another blow struck and invisible fingers wrenched my hair and raked my arms.

Ben stumbled up towards me and scooped me off the floor. Lights flickered and doors slammed and flew open. He dropped me onto my bed, and collapsed across me as his legs gave way. The bedroom door slammed and flew open, rebounded from the wall and banged shut.

An uneasy silence followed.

I twisted out from beneath him, hugged my knees to my chest and sobbed. He curled against me and wrapped his arms around me. "Come stay at mine, please. You're not safe here."

"This is my home. I'm not leaving. Vincent is trying to tell me something but I'm too stupid to figure out what."

"This is not Vincent. It's this place. There's always been something wrong here. The guy who bought the property paid good money for the rebuild. Then one day he came to the site to check on progress and something scared the shit out of him. He paid me to finish the job then sold the house. He never came back, not even for me to hand over the keys."

We dozed and talked in restless bouts, and fell asleep soon after Shelly arrived home. Deep in the night wind plucked at the plastic sheeting and woke me from a nightmare. Ben shifted and I turned to face him. He drew me close and his lips brushed mine, a moth-wing touch which sent a frisson of heat coursing through me. We'd arrived at the inexorable moment which would alter the course of our relationship, and I knew with every ounce of my being this beautiful thing about to happen would, in time, fester into the ugliness which always consumed any promise of contentment.

We woke, tangled. I couldn't bear to move and lose his warmth so clung to him for as long as possible. A sunbeam divided the room. Our discarded clothing lay strewn over the floor and, in the corner by the wardrobe, sat the photo frame of Dorothy and Vincent's baby.

"Good morning." Ben buried his face in the curve of my neck and tickled me with his breath. "We have serious matters to discuss, Madame," he teased, "but first, coffee." He rolled off the bed and walked naked to the bathroom. And returned a moment later with a towel wrapped around his waist. "Forgot about Sean."

Whilst he made coffee, I fetched the boxes from where we'd abandoned them downstairs. The morning sun drenched the floors and walls with light and eradicated the slightest shadow, yet I bore a mask of confidence I didn't feel, and dread gnawed at my nerves.

I nestled into the duvet and tidied the boxes. Ben brought our coffees and snuggled in. He caught a tear as it slid off my cheek, and cradled my head on his shoulder. I wept. For Dorothy and her lost baby, and for Vincent's unquiet soul. And for myself, and the inescapable misery which was my life.

Chapter 12

I hated Christmas. I hated that when I thought about Christmas my mother's face appeared in my head to remind me I'd not called her. Along with the drudge of shopping came the burden of decorating, and cooking, and feeling obliged to be nice, or be judged.

I hadn't thought to reconsider Christmas angst in light of my new circumstance, and knew Father Murphy had great expectations of seeing me in the pews for his advent service. Wherever I looked, festive lights twinkled, and adorned trees peered from windows. Except for my house.

"I have to get home to see what Shelly's doing to my place." I lay face down with my head cradled in my arms as Ben's hand glided along my spine in gentle strokes. "She promised no more than a tree and lights, but you know her."

He grunted. "Has Filly invited you for Christmas day?"

"She mentioned it in passing, but didn't get into details."

"Say no. I want you all to myself." He traced the line of my jaw and kissed my eyelid. "We can hole up here, eat stuff and walk around naked all day."

"What? And give the citizens of Sleepy Hollow more to gossip about?" I did a lazy roll onto my back and stretched like a satisfied cat.

His fingertip explored my bellybutton. "I don't care about them," he said. "I care about this . . . and this . . . and this." And he showed me how much he cared about every inch of me.

Our relationship had evolved, and I'd swapped my bed for his to avoid Shelly's supercilious scrutiny. As a result, I faced an almost daily walk of shame which I pretended no one in the neighbourhood noticed, least of all Father Murphy on his morning errands.

On weekends we escaped through the garden gate into the fields for walks, or we drove to St Agnes for fish and chips. We often spoke long into the night, made love, laughed until we ached, and found companionship in our moments of silence.

I showered and dressed, and Ben watched from the gate as I trudged through slush left over from a snow flurry the night before. I cut through the churchyard and crossed the intersection. As I turned the corner, I spied Bill and

Shelly arguing on my driveway and retreated enough to watch, unobserved from around the hedgerow.

I strained to hear. Bill gesticulated and Shelly countered with her own series of arm movements. For several heartbeats they glared at one another. Then Bill got in his car and sped off down the road. Shelly stood, arms folded, and stared after him.

I gave her a few minutes to get inside before I turned the corner. Inside, I found her fussing with tree lights, and she cursed when they tumbled out of the box and unravelled at her feet. "Need help?"

"Nah. Stupid things always get in a tangle," she said. "I could do with a stepladder though." She stood aside, and waited for my assessment of our tree. She'd been crying. Beneath spider lashes her red-rimmed eyes glistened.

"How did you get this beast home?" I settled into the Papasan chair she'd shifted to make room for the biggest tree in the forest.

"Kenver's doing deliveries. He's got a couple of trees for sale outside the pub." With a dramatic flourish she showed off an array of decorations in silvers and pinks. "And these came this morning." She finished off with a pirouette.

"I'll get the ladder, you make the coffees."

"Hold that thought," she said. "I'm on the lunch shift to pay for this baby. But tonight I'm yours. . ." She made one final twirl and sang as she put on her boots and coat.

I swept up pine needles and examined her decorations,

impressed she'd gone for sophisticated when I'd expected gaudy. I felt none of her enthusiasm, but promised myself I'd be more considerate towards her and not dampen her excitement.

I had an hour to spare before my appointment to go through the church records with Father Murphy. I booted my laptop, checked emails, and loaded my latest article to edit. I made yet another mental note to call my mother, though I'd ignored each one for the past three weeks and risked falling outside Rachel's domestic statute of limitations on being ignored.

A knock on the door drew me out of my reverie. I saved my changes and made my way downstairs. Through the door's peephole I squizzed Bill and frowned. Bill?

"Veronica, Hi." He glanced over his shoulder before he stepped inside. "Do you have a minute?"

I looked too, not sure who he'd expected to see lurking on the drive. "I do. Shall I pop the kettle on?"

"No." He touched my elbow then shrunk back. "I can't stay."

I gestured for him to sit, and I perched on the edge of the sofa. Bill had a mild manner, soft greying hair and gentle features, though a range of emotions flitted across his face and he licked his lips. "Are you here for gift ideas for Elaine?" Daft question. What else could he want to speak to me about?

"I'm sorry, truly," he said, "but you need to know . . . about Sean. And the others." He checked his watch, then his eyes roamed the room. "I've waited too long, but enough's enough." He took a breath and stood, plunged his hands into his trouser pockets and paced. "I promised myself I'd keep my nose out of their business, but you don't deserve this." He sat again and fidgeted. "Sean's a bad egg, Veronica. Always has been. Nothing he does is without purpose, and lodging here with you is not by accident."

My gut clenched. I watched Bill's features, searched for a clue to his meaning.

He grabbed his knees. "He's easily manipulated. There's no loyalty, no common decency even."

Realisation dawned, staring me in the face all this time. "You're Shelly's father?"

He snorted.

"She told me she'd come here to live with her father." No one had bothered to mention Bill was Shelly's father.

"Then you'll know the rest, about why I left him and his mother."

"Not really. It's not my business, Bill." The judgement I'd formulated for Shelly's evil father seemed unsuited to the doleful man sat before me.

He lowered his head and coughed, or sobbed, I couldn't tell which. I maintained the silence, not for the sake of further revelation, but because I had no idea how to react.

"How does a parent deal with something so terrifying? One minute I've got a son, then he comes out as gay, then five minutes later he decides he's not gay, he's transgender. Now he's a her not a him. My head's spinning." He pinched the bridge of his nose. "I can't talk to him. I don't know who he is. He's always been resentful and nasty.

"He arrived here out the blue and demanded money for surgery, and for his rent to be paid, and he doesn't stop, one thing after another. I'd been with Elaine for four years. I'd never told her about Sean's condition, she just knew I had a son somewhere in the world. He sidled in, latched on to her, and now, he's parading around like one of the girls whilst I'm having to foot the bill and explain great big wodges spent on the credit cards."

He stood, and sat back down.

"Bill, I can understand you being confused, but being trans is not a condition. Shelly's not ill, she has gender dysphoria. You need to speak to a professional, see if they can help you understand her, or bring you together to talk about what she's going through. This is serious stuff and you need to tell Elaine about the money. Keeping secrets is leaving you open to coercion."

He nodded, slow wretched bobs of his head. "I couldn't bear to lose her."

I almost thought he meant Shelly. "I don't imagine Elaine's someone who'd be so flaky," I said, without conviction. "You need to come clean with her. If she can't support you through this then what's she really worth to you? If you both stand together then Shelly has no leverage."

He straightened his shoulders and pulled a handkerchief from his pocket. "I'm sorry, Veronica. You're right, of course, but life's not clear cut."

Not by a long shot, matey.

He blew his nose. "I didn't come to unload this on you. What I wanted to say is you need to watch yourself. Your so-called friends aren't what they seem."

Anxiety settled like stone in the pit of my belly. "What do you mean?"

He stood and tucked away the hanky, and I hoped he wasn't going to offer to shake my hand. He ambled to the door. "They're not your friends, Veronica, not one of them. Sean's their puppet, doing their bidding and conspiring against you. Right from the start, since you first arrived, they've been scheming. I've told Ben numerous times to watch out for you, but he's involved too, which makes it difficult for him to take sides." He let himself out, hurried down the drive and got into his car.

"Wait. Why?" I chased after him. "Conspiring about what?" What was Ben involved in and why did he have to take sides? Bill gave me a wan look as he reversed out the drive. "Bill, please."

I watched his taillights disappear around the corner and spotted Father Murphy watching me from the churchyard. Shit. I checked my watch. I turned to go inside, and the door swung shut before I made it to the top step.

I leaned into the light and examined my face in the bathroom mirror. Ben sat on the bed and tied his bootlaces. He seemed preoccupied and I wondered, for the hundredth time, whether I should tell him about Bill's visit. I stalled, not for my own benefit, rather for the sake of keeping the peace with Shelly.

He came to me and wrapped me in his arms. "See you tonight and you can tell me what you found in the church records?" He planted a kiss on the tip of my nose and his fingers slid over my breast and tweaked my nipple.

"Is everything okay?" I said. "You're brooding."

He took a deep breath and his chest expanded. His heartbeat thumped in my ear. "Tracy's invited me around to hers to talk. Gareth's in London."

What? I'd been so engrossed in Ben I'd almost forgotten the horrid woman existed. "Are you going?"

He relaxed his embrace and sighed. "This afternoon. If I don't go, she'll keep pestering me and then start on you. I don't want you caught up in this, Vee. I need to deal with her and get her off my back."

All warmth drained from me. I shrugged out of his arms and stepped away from him. How many times would it take for me to learn? A wave of nausea engulfed me and I gripped the edge of the hand basin. "How convenient for you both to have Gareth out the way."

He put up no argument. He stood behind me and

stared at me in the mirror. Bill's words clanged like a fire bell in my head. "You're still involved with her."

He shook his head. "Where's this coming from? Have I said or done anything to make you doubt me?"

I wanted to hurt him. I clung to the porcelain. "You're going to go to her house, whilst Gareth's away, to chat. Doesn't that sound wrong to you?"

His hands circled my waist. "I know how it sounds. But I need you to trust me. Please."

Trust. A gallant word stuck somewhere in the dictionary between slut and unfaithful.

"She's possessive, and until she lets go of me we're going to keep going around in circles." He kissed my shoulder. "I'll see you later.

CHAPTER 13

I SKULKED BENEATH THE RAG TREE, alone in the gloom, the sky overhead as heavy as my heart. Twice in as many days, I'd followed Vincent to the tree in hope of a clue, but each time he blinked out gazing into the branches. Stare all I want, each rag looked as insignificant and morose as the next.

"Son-of-a-bitch." My voice rebounded, flat, like a cold slap. I slip-slid to the roadside and stamped mud off my boots. My house and the woods had become oppressive, and on bad days too much to bear. Shelly's plan to spend Christmas in London with Dan meant I'd soon be alone.

I pressed my thumb knuckles into my eye sockets and my gloves soaked up my tears.

"Sounds kind of personal." Gareth's voice shocked the life out of me. His dog tangled herself around my legs and I stumbled against him. He gripped my shoulders and held me at arm's length. "Bit early to be staggering around out here."

"What do you care?" I bent and scratched the Labrador's ears. She nuzzled my neck and I clung to her warmth. Of all people to bump into. When I straightened, his eyes fixed on mine, his mouth a hard line.

He gave his head a micro shake. "You're brave. And stupid."

"What's that supposed to mean?"

He glanced at the tree and sighed. "What is it you're hoping to find out here? Trust me, there's nothing but lost causes and sorrow."

Story of my life.

He turned around, took a few steps, and stopped. "Get out of that house. You're going to get hurt."

An odd thought struck me. "Where are you going? You don't have to change the direction of your walk because of me."

"I'm heading home. I've come too far anyway."

I looked from him to the tree, then down the road to nowhere. "Where's home?"

"Seafarer's Cottage, the B&B," he said.

"Why are you so obnoxious with me?"

He marched right up to me, so close I could smell fabric softener and dog on him. "I'm not obnoxious. I'm furious. I know who you are, girlie. You can fool them all you want, but I know."

I stepped away from him. My knees trembled.

"Why in God's name you bought the place is beyond me." He scratched his head and bunched a tuft of hair in his fist. "Have you got a death wish? What do you want to prove?"

"What are you talking about?"

He did a three-sixty degree turn in the road. His dog's tail wagged, excited by the new game, and she followed him in a wide circle, tongue lolling. "I can't believe Rachel let you come here without warning you."

My mother's name came like a punch in the stomach. He knew my mother.

"The stupid bitch." He lunged towards me.

I flinched and extended my hands to halt his charge. "She doesn't know I'm here."

"Go home to your spoilt brat life and leave us alone." He wrenched the dog's leash and they strode away. Home to Tracy. On the road to nowhere. Ben's road to nowhere.

I cried all the way home. On my top step, I took a deep breath to calm my nerves and let myself in. Pink and silver baubles lay strewn across the room. I kicked the one nearest my foot and relished the sound as the fragile sphere splintered against the wall. "Damn right I have something to prove." I plucked my phone from my pocket, nipped my glove between my teeth and tugged it off, and prodded the screen.

I held the phone to my ear and launched another bauble through the kitchen doorway. The bauble shot back through the air and shattered against the door behind me.

"Is that the best you can do, you fucker?"

"Roo? I'd abandoned all hope of hearing from you." Rachel. Sweet as antifreeze. "Who are you shouting at?"

The tree shivered and several baubles fell and bounced in all directions. The fairy lights cable twitched and slithered slow as a snake between the branches. I had a sudden urge to pee. I wrenched the front door open and dashed outside to stand on the driveway.

"Roo? Talk to me."

"I'm in Cornwall, Mum." The line went silent. I watched the door and window for movement. "Mum?" In any other circumstance, I'd have relished the opportunity to leave my mother speechless.

"What in God's name . . . tell me exactly where you are?"

"At the moment I'm on my driveway. My house is possessed by a homicidal ghost. And then this fat asshole with a whore wife tells me I don't belong."

Rachel shouted in my ear. "Stop screaming, I can't hear a word you're saying."

"And guess what, Mum, he says you should have warned me not to come here. You. Rachel. I haven't told anyone who I am. But he knows. He knows us."

The door shuddered, slammed and sprang open. A fractured bauble bounced out and rolled to my feet, accompanied by the acrid stench of burnt hair. I cancelled the call and sprinted through the gate into the back yard. Shelly's curtains were drawn, no flames. The back door squeaked on its hinges, swung open and slammed. On the inside, the key slid out the lock and dropped to the floor.

My body trembled. I couldn't do this anymore. I slid down the wall and sat on the cold ground. My phone bleeped. I fumbled with my glove and answered.

"Roo, listen carefully. If this is about spiting me, you need to stop."

"Why is everything always about you?" I sobbed into the crook of my arm.

"Pack your things and come home. We can talk about this. You can sell the damned house and I don't care where you go, anywhere but Cornwall. Please darling. Please come home. Today."

"No. I can sort this out. I need to understand what he wants."

"What who wants? Roo, you're not making sense."

"Vincent. Something to do with the tree. But I can't figure out what." I used my glove to wipe my nose.

"Oh dear God." Rachel hyperventilated on the other end. "I don't know what to do for you. I'm so far away."

"Do nothing, Mum. This is my life. I chose to come here. Daddy always said he wanted to come home, I've come home for him. I just need to sort out Vincent."

"No. You don't understand. Your father didn't leave because he wanted to. We had no choice. You're putting yourself in unnecessary danger."

"I'm tired. I need to go." I ended the call and sat with my head in my arms. My teeth chattered from cold, and fear. "Vincent?" I lifted my head and shouted. "Tell me what you want, you moron."

The door opened and startled me. Ben stepped out. "You're going to make yourself sick out here. Who are you shouting at?" He helped me to my feet and wiped sticky tears and snot off my face. "What the hell's going on?"

"How did you get inside?"

"The front door's wide open. And Sean's going to be pissed when he sees what you've done to his tree." I resisted him on the doorstep and his eyebrows drew together. "Come inside, Vee. I'm here with you."

"Stop calling me Vee, it sounds ridiculous."

He closed the door behind me and helped me out of my coat. All the while, he contemplated. "Anything or anyone else you want to have a go at?" He snapped the switch on the kettle, lifted two mugs off the drying rack, and leaned against the counter with his arms crossed.

I could think of a few. I gave him my finest death stare.

He laughed. "Give it your best shot. I've got nothing to hide from you."

"You didn't say Tracy owns the B&B. The night at the tree, you'd been with her."

"Like I say, I've got nothing to hide."

I wanted to punch him in the face. "Bill came round the other day," I said. "He says you're still involved. And you're all conspiring against me. Why? What have I done to you?"

He scowled. "Bill's got a big mouth," he said. "And I've warned you enough times about Sean. He's a little shit and stirs trouble wherever he goes."

"I don't care. I want to know about you. What's your part in everything?"

"I don't have a part. I'm with you because I want to be."

"Because you chose me?"

He narrowed his eyes. "What are you asking me?"

"Did you choose me? Are you on my side?"

"Side? Against what?"

"Or are you so involved that you can't choose sides because you want both."

A muscle twitched in his jaw. "What are you talking about?"

A door banged upstairs and hives broke out on my neck. I shook my head. "I don't know. I'm tired. Sick to death." Tears brimmed. "I wanted a second chance, to have my own life where no one's manipulating me and demeaning everything I do. I hoped with you things would be different. I'm such an idiot."

The kettle clicked off and the wall plug sparked. Smoke seeped from the socket and billowed behind Ben. A face emerged through swirling eddies, looking straight at me. The mouth opened in a scream.

I clamped my hands over my ears and cowered. Damp warmth gushed out of my nostrils and mouth and fat red drops dripped onto the floor. Ben shouted but his words made no sense above the shrieking. He gripped my wrists and shook me. His mouth moved, formed words. He placed his hands over mine, clamped my head and fixed his eyes on mine, intense, hazel irises shot with gold.

Shrieks quelled to wails. He held on. Focused pinpoint pupils.

Wails abated to whimpers.

Then silence.

He placed paper towel under my nose, led me to the sink, and ran cold water. I washed my face and the water turned pink. He turned off the tap and fresh blood dripped onto the smooth stone and formed a gelatinous stream which slithered down the plughole.

A ray of afternoon sunlight permeated the curtains and roused me. My consciousness chased a dream fragment, which escaped into sleep's murky realm. Through waking fug came voices. I tugged a pillow over my head and anxiety welled from my stomach and made my chest ache. I raised myself on my elbows and listened.

Curiosity got the better of me and I slid off the bed. I tiptoed to the door and across the hallway to the top of the stairs, but the voices receded. I snuck to my bedroom window and peeped out, enough to see the driveway.

Tracy leaned against her car, breasts perky, hips jutted in a suggestive pose, and smirked. I couldn't see Ben without leaning further forward and drawing attention to myself. Her voice didn't carry, but her body language conveyed meaning. She reached out and he placed a set of keys in her palm.

A flare of indignation warmed my core and I willed her to touch him, to justify my distrust. She got in her car and started the engine. The window slid open and Ben leaned in. I couldn't see their faces, didn't know what they were doing. When she reversed out of the drive, I watched Ben watch her go.

CHAPTER 14

Father Murphy looked pleased with himself. "Baptism, marriage and burial records at your disposal." Three piles awaited my scrutiny. He'd provided a notebook and mechanical pencil, and a steaming mug of tea. He hovered inside the door whilst I placed my laptop on the desk and hung my jacket and bag on the coat stand. "Shout if there's anything you need," he said. "I'm rehearsing my sermon."

Six days until Christmas. Seven weeks had passed in a blink. In less than two months my life and I had transformed beyond recognition. I'd accomplished an escape from tyranny, and though I'd dreamed of peace and quiet, and time to heal, I couldn't remember the last time I'd achieved any desired outcomes.

He'd placed the registers in descending date order. Most appeared to be in good condition, whilst the older ones suffered black speckled mildew and smelled musty. I lifted the nearest cover and leafed through. Each page listed eight entries. I squinted at the handwriting and closed the book. I booted my laptop and opened the document I'd created for my research notes.

My search focused on three families, Mackie, Killigrew and Hendry. The registers in front of me covered the period nineteen hundred to nineteen sixty-five. On my previous visit I'd searched marriages through to nineteen forty. No Gladys Hendry. No Hendrys at all. I had two Killigrews listed, but both too late to account for Dorothy's birth.

I piled the unwanted registers on the table's far corner and focused on marriages between nineteen forty and nineteen fifty. Whilst I read and made notes, the watery sun ascended to the window's height and disappeared over the rooftop, depriving the room of warmth and cheer. Around midday Father Murphy's head appeared round the door and he offered me tea and a sandwich.

We sat in the Vicarage's front room. Crimson carpet, scarlet lounge suite, dark wood furnishings, vermilion curtains with beige lining and gold tassel tie backs. On the walls, pasty biblical images in gold frames which denoted their age, and the Queen, staid in a bygone era. I wondered at Father Murphy's bright disposition. Faced with his décor I'd have developed a psychosis.

"How's the research going?" He balanced his plate on his knees and nibbled off his side crusts, followed by a sip of tea.

"Marriages are a bit of a dead end. I've found Arthur Mackie's marriage to May Errington. That's nineteen forty-four. I'm mid-way through nineteen forty-nine so I'll finish off nineteen fifty and move on to baptisms."

He puckered his lips and adjusted his glasses. "Perhaps you'll have better luck with baptisms and burials. You see, the Mackies go back a way, but Arthur had one daughter and no brothers, so no sons were produced."

I took him to mean the Mackie name might not have lived on, but perhaps their blood still flowed strong.

He proceeded to nibble off the residual crust. "Any luck with old Arthur?"

"I heard he's been in hospital, and Elaine didn't want to impose with him being so ill."

Father Murphy crinkled his nose and frowned. "Arthur had a hospital appointment a couple of weeks ago, I know that much, but he's not been ill as far as I'm aware. I spotted him going into the Old Mill yesterday morning." He considered his words and his brows twitched. "Oh dear."

Not the phrase I'd have used. My tea scalded my throat but did little to dampen my fury. The room, which a moment ago lacked sufficient warmth, felt stifling. "Maybe I'll make my own enquiries."

He gave a slow nod and munched through his sandwich like he wished he could eat his words instead of ham and cheese.

Half an hour later I resumed with marriages since nineteen forty-nine and found nothing notable. I had a handful of names and a crick in my neck, and I needed a pee. I checked the time. The records for nineteen fifty covered fewer pages than the previous years. I could finish off and make a start on burials with enough time to get to the Old Mill for the end of Shelly's shift and buy us dinner.

In the February of nineteen fifty the handwriting changed and I had to decipher the new scrawl. A familiar flow of surnames filled the pages, with occasional new ones fetching in fresh blood. Ben hadn't been kidding when he'd said much of the community were related in some way. May of nineteen fifty produced four entries. I skimmed over the first two. My eyes settled on the third entry and my heart fluttered. I reread the entry and typed the groom's details into my notes. I touched a fingertip to the bride's name.

Alice Mackie. Age twenty. Her place of residence stated The Vicarage. Bride's father, The Reverend, George Mackie. I typed Alice's details in the column next to her husband's and highlighted the entry. I ran the cursor to the column with Arthur Mackie's entry and highlighted the section. Arthur and Alice shared a father and a residence.

I continued with marriages into the nineteen sixties and discovered an entry in nineteen sixty-four for Georgina Mackie, daughter of Arthur and May. I compared notes with Alice Mackie and although twelve years separated their marriages, a connection existed between their husbands. The Mackie name did desist, but two Mackie girls, Arthur's sister and daughter, both married Marshalls.

My fingers hovered, unsteady, above the keyboard. I typed a footnote and reclined. The implications of my discovery weren't lost on me. I separated the registers into complete and pending piles and selected the burial register containing entries from nineteen thirty.

January recorded two burials. I turned the page and scanned through February. My blood pressure spiked. Name of deceased, Vincent Mackie. Aged seventeen. Eldest son of The Reverend, George Mackie, and Mrs Gladys Hendry.

My body tingled and goosebumps prickled on my arms and neck. I lay both hands, palms down on the pages, as if I could communicate with Vincent through the ink. I'd found him. And I'd found Gladys Hendry. If his burial had been conducted in this church then his grave might be somewhere in the grounds. I placed a marker in the register, took my phone out of my bag and photographed a close up of Vincent's entry. I left the office and followed the sound of Father Murphy's voice.

He waved me across and closed his bible. "Are you off?"

"No. I didn't mean to disturb you, but how do I find a grave?"

He descended from the pulpit and adjusted his sleeves. "We can take a look. The records are online.

All you need is a surname, and once you've located the plot number it's a matter of checking the location on the churchyard map. Anyone in particular?"

"Vincent Mackie. His burial took place in nineteen thirty."

"Ah yes." He led the way to the office and stood beside me whilst I entered the church's URL into Google. A basic web page opened, with creepy little black headstones to click on instead of links. "First the surname index."

I located surname index LUM – NOR. Beneath each surname appeared a list of first name, age, date of burial and plot number. Mackies occupied several columns, listed in burial date order. I scrolled to the nineteen hundreds and scanned the names until I found Vincent. I jotted down his plot number and closed the web page.

The churchyard plan opened to an aerial photograph, taken on a sunny summer day, showing the rooftops of the church and nearby surroundings. I recognised the Old Mill, and Ben's row of houses. My eyes followed the road past the intersection, and instead of my house I discovered a segment of property on which stood the ruined mill and haphazard foundations flanked by the woods. My throat constricted and an icy tendril of unease rippled between my shoulder blades, akin to a premonition. I scrolled through the yard plan's five burial plots.

"You'll take ages to find it on this," Father Murphy said. "Try the burial stone location, that will tell you which plot the grave is in with a grid reference.

I dropped down the plan and loaded the index. I scrolled to 391. "Plot 1, grid reference E3." I returned to the plan, found the plot and followed the grid reference. Vincent's grave lay with nine others on a triangle of land on the church's northeast side. I scrolled to the photograph and located the spot. Vincent lay less than five metres from the path which cut through the churchyard. For almost two months I'd walked past his grave.

I shut my laptop and packed it away, tugged on my jacket, and slung my bag across my shoulder. Father Murphy straightened the registers and studied my face. "Will you still be needing any of these?"

I patted the pending piles. "Yes, these please." I paused at the door. "Thank you for allowing me to go through your records."

"May I ask," he said, "what your interest is in Vincent Mackie?"

Yes of course, Father, he's a badass ghost who's haunting my house and scaring the shit out of me. "You'll probably not believe me," I said.

He perched on the table's corner. "Try me."

I gave him an abridged version of Vincent's escapades and flits to the rag tree. He neither smirked, nor did he show a flicker of disbelief. "I wish I could understand what he's trying to tell me. I love my home, but if I'm honest, he's winning this battle."

"I could do a blessing," he said. "If you're comfortable with the notion."

I doubted a bit of holy water would dispel Vincent's tantrums. "Sure, why not. I have some of his things, like the tie he wore the day he died." I shuddered. "Maybe you could bless those too. Perhaps he's attached to them."

Now his eyes twinkled. "Where did you get these items?"

"I found a box in my attic, and Felicity's sister, Colette, sent over another box. I've got letters and photographs, Vincent's tie, and there's a tin of bits and pieces. And a ring."

Father Murphy scratched his chin. "How do you know he wore the tie the day of his death?"

"There's a letter from Vincent's mother. She placed the tie in the rag tree and Vincent's . . . girlfriend or fiancé, Dorothy, took it as a keepsake."

His face drained of colour. "Dorothy Killigrew."

"Yes."

"And you possess the tie." He walked to the window and stood, hands behind his back. He rocked on his heels. "I may have an inkling as to the message young Vincent is conveying."

He needn't have gone any further. The idea struck like a lightning bolt. "Bloody hell, all this time. God, I'm so thick." I bit my lip. "Sorry."

"Perhaps if you return the tie to the tree you'll set your conscience at rest and find the peace you seek."

My conscience? For a moment he'd convinced me he believed in Vincent. I swallowed a retort. This wasn't my first spin on the merry-go-round. My mother would love this. I'd conjured my own haunting to torment my conscience.

"I'm heading off," I said.

"I'll call you to arrange the blessing, and another viewing appointment, but you're looking at mid-January," he said.

I'd lost my appetite and my insides churned with terrible excitement. Instead of heading to the pub I followed the path to the northeast gate and stepped onto the frozen grass. Vincent's gravestone resembled several of those which surrounded his, an unremarkable grey headstone bearing his name, the date of his birth and demise, and an epitaph. "Beloved son, the Lord's to keep, we bid you now a blessed sleep."

A soul forgotten. I crouched and touched the cold stone. "I know what to do now, Vincent."

CHAPTER 15

WAVES OF NAUSEA SUBSIDED. I clung to the toilet seat and lay for a while with my head on my arms. I flushed, but when I attempted to stand the room rocked like a storm ravaged ship. I crawled to the bath to rinse my mouth, gulped a mouthful of cold water, and washed my face.

Dappled sunlight streamed through the frosted window and gleamed off the tiles. I swallowed bile and bitter fear, gathered my duvet and pillow, and opened the bathroom door a crack. I braced myself to look out. My clothes and shoes lay strewn across the floor and the baby faced me from within her photo frame, positioned in my bedroom doorway.

Shelly appeared, all auburn curls and pink silk dressing gown, with a face like thunder. "Are you done hogging the bathroom? I'm going to be late for work."

I snorted at the hilarity of the moment, at Shelly's

expression, undaunted by the house's state and unconcerned I'd spent the night in the bathroom under demonic missile attack. "All yours, Princess."

I dressed and waited for her in the kitchen. When she entered, I slid a mug of coffee across the counter and stood, arms folded. She plunged into the fridge and came out with a yoghurt, peeled the seal and dipped a teaspoon in.

"We need to talk," I said.

She scooped a dollop and upended the teaspoon on her tongue. "What about?"

Since Bill's visit I'd played out this moment in my head, but I knew, no matter how I mapped the conversation, things wouldn't go to plan. "Bill came to see me the other day."

The spoon stalled on her tongue and her eyes snapped to meet mine. "What for?"

"To talk about you."

She jabbed the spoon into the yoghurt tub and flung them into the sink. "So, what, now you're going to throw me out. Like everyone else has?"

"I'm not throwing you out. I want you to know what he said so I can get your side."

She stormed out the kitchen and stomped around the dining table snarling. The hard face she'd upheld over the past few days cracked and somehow broke. Her mouth slackened and tears and spit mingled and dropped in strings onto her blouse. She squatted with her back to the wall, buried her head in her arms and sobbed.

I dragged a chair from beneath the table and sat. Temper tantrums were my forte. I had lots of experience and knew best to wait out the storm. She raged. After half an hour I went for my phone and rang Kenver to say she'd woken with a migraine and would be late for her shift. Between sobs she regurgitated a wailing rendition of her life. I'd heard the pathos a dozen times and waited until her cries simmered to chokes before I sat beside her and slung an arm around her.

"You're a good person," she said. She lifted her head and wiped her nose on her sleeve. "I totally don't deserve you." I fetched paper towel, and whilst I made us coffees she abandoned her jacket and shoes and migrated to the lounge.

I handed her a mug and sank into the sofa next to her. She plucked off her soggy lashes and flicked them onto the coffee table. "I'm probably sacked as well as homeless now."

I did a mental eye roll. "I phoned you in sick."

"What did the old fuck father of mine say about me? Did he dead-name me?" She folded her feet beneath her and sipped her coffee.

"Yes, he did, and he said nothing I haven't heard before. He said you and the others are conspiring against me. He seems to think you're being manipulated by them."

She scratched a spot on her knee until a tiny bead of blood formed. "Do I look like a person who lets people manipulate me?"

"Is it Tracy?"

She sniffed. "Tracy's a nothing. All she wants is Ben. How's manipulating me going to fix that?"

"Bill says Ben's involved in this conspiracy."

She shot me a look and returned to her picking. "What conspiracy? Ben's got nothing to do with anything. He's not the problem."

"I want to know what's going on. I thought you guys were my friends, but now I'm confused. Have I done something to upset you all?"

"Bill's full of shit," she said. "He's trying to make trouble for me."

"Because you're blackmailing him?"

She jumped to her feet and spilled coffee on herself. "I've asked for nothing more than what I deserve from my father. He left us. He broke my mother's heart." She set her mug down, sat and covered her face with her hands. "He broke my heart."

Short of waterboarding, I got nothing more out of her. She changed her shirt and left for work, and I drove to the woods. I parked on the verge and though daylight cut through the thickets, the rag tree and its vestiges lurked in shadow. Some days the woods huddled around the tree to prevent light entering, other days they loomed like sentinels warding off intruders.

No amount of time spent in the tree's vicinity eased the feeling of desolation and impending doom. Or the sensation of hundreds of pairs of spectral eyes watching, waiting. Waiting for what? As long as the tree tethered the souls interned by love, sorrow, guilt or tragedy there would be no peace.

Had Dorothy's removal of Vincent's tie meant she'd bound him to always walk the path from the tree to the house? Had he wandered through the ruins, night after night, searching for his tether?

I struggled with another notion. How had the shoebox got into my ceiling? Ben said he'd built the house from a ruin. Someone had to have put the box there for me to find, perhaps after the storm damaged my roof, when the ladder provided opportunity. And the noises, and footsteps? Vincent's tie?

I grasped the steering wheel. Condensation smudged the windows and my vision blurred. A rap on my window sent my heart ricocheting around my chest. I swiped tears off my cheeks with shaky fingers and opened the window.

"What are you doing here?" Tracy glanced around the interior and smirked. "Did you sleep in your car?" The Labrador's paws rested on the door and her tail wagged her body. She air licked me and whined until I stroked the soft fur between her ears. "Get out. Walk with me."

Had I felt any less unstable I'd have saluted the bitch. I cut the engine, zipped my jacket, and shoved my hands into my gloves. She stood at the road's edge and watched me cross.

"Gareth thinks you have a death wish living in that

house." She called the dog to heel and we walked along the verge. "I'll be honest, I've never experienced anything myself. I spent the night once, just after the carpets were laid." A lifetime of torture at the sharp end of my mother's tongue did little to help dampen the hurt Tracy's words inflicted. I'd let my feelings for Ben soften me. "All this hocus pocus and boxes and love letters and mumbo jumbo." She talked in time with her steps, slow, deliberate.

My own impotent words hid behind my tongue.

"I mean, baby photos which move around the house, and your ghost, what's his name? I think you're using the house's history as an excuse to create your own little fantasy world, and you're dragging Ben along with you."

I stopped. My heels sank in the wet grass. My mission had been to plan Vincent's release. To take time to make some sort of peace with this horrible place and figure out how to go about the ritual. I needed this time to decide whether to do this alone, or to seek Father Murphy's spiritual aid, in whatever form it was extended.

What I didn't need was to be intimidated and humiliated.

Tracy realised I'd stopped and turned. A nasty smile twisted her mouth. "The only reason he tolerates you is because he pities you. But that's Ben, always attracted to the damsel in distress. He wants to play knight in shining armour and you're providing ample opportunity." She came towards me. "It won't be long before he sees right through you, crazy little rich girl. You don't have what it takes to keep a man like him satisfied."

Her fragrance clogged my nostrils. Bile burned my throat. My stomach heaved from the rancid blend of perfume, damp ground and rotting fabric. And fear. Fear of the godforsaken tree's hideous decorations. Fear of losing control of my second chance at a life. Fear of her.

I smacked her and the sound cracked the silence. She staggered and pressed a hand to her cheek. In the split second between shock and realisation, the scald of justice burned in my chest and stomach. "If you're such an expert at everything why are you here convincing me I'm the failure?"

We glared at one another. I braced myself for retaliation, but her glance flicked past me to the tree and her features hardened. "Give it time," she said. "He will come back to me. He always does. You wait and see."

A clamour of rooks settled on the uppermost branches and rearranged their charcoal plumage. The dog barked and they erupted into the sky. All but one. One for sorrow...

Ben leaned against the worktop with his arms folded across his chest. He'd changed out of his work overalls, but his hair and eyebrows were covered in fine sawdust and he looked tired. I turned off the stove and pierced a noodle to test. He bit the noodle off the fork and sucked in air to cool his mouth.

"The idea to return Vincent's tie to the tree came from Father Murphy," I said. "I'm keen to try." I stabbed another noodle and waggled it on the fork.

"Fine, but can we do the deed in daylight? Every time we go to the tree, we're stumbling around in the pitch dark falling over the roots."

I laughed. "What do we tell the others?"

Ben grumbled. "Nothing. Leave them out of this. If your plan goes tits up and Vincent's in a rage, someone could get hurt."

"How about sunrise tomorrow? I want to get this over with."

"Do what you feel is right." He pushed himself away from the worktop, encircled me in his arms and rested his chin on my head. Despite Tracy's threats, he felt so good, so warm and steadfast.

"I spoke to Shelly this morning," I said. I clamped a noodle between my teeth. "Told her about Bill but didn't get much out of her."

"Isn't he supposed to be going to London?" His mouth covered mine and he stole my noodle.

"Cheat." I tipped the pasta into a colander to drain and gave the sauce a stir. "Dan's picking her up tomorrow."

He nuzzled my ear. "Good. We can walk around naked and take showers together."

"Is that all you think about?" I gave him a shove and dished up.

He carried our plates to the lounge. I fetched the salad. "Not at all," he said. "I think about things like staying in bed until lunchtime. Did I mention walking around naked?"

We selected a Netflix movie, and ate. I contemplated telling him about Tracy, but my wound still seeped with self-pity and I had little strength for lies. His or mine.

Come the morning, I would untether Vincent's spirit. Then I'd clean house.

One exorcism at a time.

CHAPTER 16

FROM SHELLY'S BEDROOM WINDOW I had a clear view of the back garden and the woods. The rising sun crowned the trees and the ruin's topmost point. Incessant rain had delayed my bid for Vincent's liberation, but I caught sight of movement in the woods and a pang of excitement gripped me.

I woke Ben and we dressed. I fetched Vincent's tie from the shoebox and we stepped out of the door into a frost-crusted world. Ice crunched beneath our shoes, and our breaths plumed. I held the folded tie, like clutching a handful of death.

"Do you see him?" Ben said.

Last night, whilst he'd slept, I'd stood on the path in the woods, beneath a clear sky and a slither of moon, and summoned Vincent. I didn't fear him outside the house. A lack of walls calmed his frenetic spirit. He hadn't appeared on command. Instead, after a long while, I'd sensed him, and his aura flickered amongst the trees not far from me. There had been much I wanted to say to him, but I gave a fleeting explanation, uncertain whether my words fell on non-existent ears.

At the treeline, beyond the sun's glare, stood Vincent clutching his boater. No longer a grainy flickering phantom, his essence glowed with the intensity of the winter sun. "Yes. He's waiting for us," I said.

We passed between trees and low-hanging branches. Ben held my hand and we followed our well-trodden path. For the first time since I'd encountered the rag tree, its branches glistened beneath the sun's touch. Tatty morsels of fabric, ribbons and scarves fluttered and quivered on a sudden gust.

Vincent stood on the spot beneath the tree, fingers fidgeting with the hat's rim, eyes fixed on the branches above. I unfurled the tie and handed it to Ben.

"Where do I put it?" he said, his voice a rasped whisper.

I pointed to where I thought Vincent gazed. "There's a gap between that teddy and the yellow ribbon."

"Do we need to say anything?" Ben said.

Vincent had been the son of a vicar. A prayer seemed appropriate, but all I had was a half remembered bedtime prayer. Ben recited the Lord's Prayer, and after we'd both muttered amen he stepped forward, careful of the roots snaking underfoot. He gave Vincent sufficient berth then reached into the tree. He wound the tie around the branch a couple of times and tied a knot, then returned to my side.

Nothing happened. Vincent's aura flickered and a spasm of panic trapped my breath. Replacing the tie hadn't worked. Then Ben gripped my wrist. Vincent stood, frozen in time. The air crackled with static, and sparks like tiny fireflies wove around us in slow iridescent murmuration. The wind gathered strength and the fiery susurrus circled Vincent until his aura blazed, the glare so intense we had to shield our eyes.

When we looked again, we stood alone beneath the rag tree. Of Vincent and the lights there remained no trace. The wind shook the tree and its trophies, and the tie clung to the branch, bright, unmarred by damp and rot.

The flesh at my nape prickled. Instead of elation, an ominous emptiness lurked. I took Ben's offered hand and we walked home the long way round, allowing time for me to process a torrent of emotions.

We reached the church, and the windows caught the sunrise. Christmas Eve. At midnight, lights would shine behind those windows as Father Murphy delivered advent mass to his dutiful congregation. We turned the bend and my house waited.

Ben waved from the fireside sofa. I elbowed my way

through the throng and emerged wearing the sweetest smile I could muster for the turncoats. Tracy and Gareth, Elaine and Bill, Felicity and Tom. The usual suspects, minus Shelly. Elaine and Filly, adorned in tinsel and glitter, giggled with Christmas merriment. Tracy's sparkle stemmed from red gloss lipstick and nails, and a see-through gold sequined blouse.

I sat next to Ben. "You look gorgeous," he said. He planted a lavish kiss on my lips and I flushed, aware of our audience's peevish glances.

Christmas choruses competed with the din of conversation. Windows fogged and daylight faded. I recognised few familiar faces in the horde, whilst Ben spent the best part of the day nodding, waving and returning shouted greetings. I had no idea so many people lived in the locality.

As the night progressed, almost every soul crammed beneath the Old Mill's beams lacked gravitas. Including me, but not sufficient to ignore Tracy and Ben's overlapped absences. My festive spirit diminished and a part of me ached like an exposed tooth cavity.

The last orders bell rang, and Kenver called time. We finished our drinks, donned our coats and scarves, and fought the crowd to exit the door in a nimbus of steam and jollification. Clusters of people staggered in the church's direction, where Father Murphy awaited his congregation in a radiance of ecclesiastical porch light.

Due to my mother's lack of religious verve, I'd

experienced Midnight Mass just once in my life. I'd been fourteen, and was permitted a sleepover at my best friend Elizabeth's. We'd accompanied her oddball parents and three obscene brothers to church. One of the boys had spilled champagne on me at supper and I'd sat in the Lord's holy house reeking of alcohol whilst they giggled like imbeciles and flapped their hands in front of their noses.

We reached the junction and I slowed. "I'm heading home," I said.

Felicity spun on her heel. "Oh no, you're not. You can't miss Midnight Mass." She waved an arm, "Everyone does Christmas Eve mass."

Ben stood silent beside me.

"I'm sure everyone will cope with my absence. See you tomorrow." I adjusted my scarf to cover my ears and crossed the road to avoid Filly's whingeing. I arrived home, and stood at my front gate until Father Murphy closed the church doors.

I knuckled tears out of my eyes and unlocked the door. I paused to gauge the atmosphere before I entered, and snapped on the light. Baubles lay scattered across the floor where I'd left them. Warmth embraced me. I shut the door and divested of my outer layer.

Whilst the congregation cantillated, I cleaned house, starting with the tree's removal. I dragged the shedding monstrosity onto the drive and left it where everyone could see. I packed Shelly's baubles and left them on her bed then sent my mother a text and turned off my phone. Prosecco and Drambuie drowned my sorrows.

Worn out and worse the wear from slanderous alcoholic salutations to Vincent's departed soul, Shelly's duplicity, and Ben's treason, I ignored the doorknocker's constant clatter and sank into warm dark oblivion, and resurfaced to find Ben at my bedside. My stomach heaved. "What do you want? What's the time?"

He sat and ran a finger along my jaw to my chin. "You abandoned me."

I kicked off the duvet and trip stumbled to the bathroom to relieve my stomach of curdled wine and whisky liqueur. My head spun and the floor reached for me. Ben's arms encircled my waist and supported me whilst I rinsed my mouth. "I don't need you. Go away. Go to Tracy."

He bent, slid an arm behind my knees, and lifted me. "So that's what this is about."

I fought him and made an ungracious descent. "That's what it's always about, Ben. I'm an idiot. Shelly warned me. Bill warned me. Tracy too." I stormed to my bedroom and slammed the door. "Go away."

I sat and gathered the covers around me and hugged my pillow. A fresh wave of nausea stung my throat. The door opened and Ben settled on the mattress next to me. "We can't build this relationship if you're going to keep throwing Tracy in my face."

"How can I trust you if you keep sneaking off with

her?"

He rubbed his eyes. "I don't sneak off with her. It's impossible to avoid her. Everything aside, we are still friends."

Friends. Indefectible confederates who outlive childhood, puberty, enemies and lovers, and stand as solemn mourners at funerals. Who needs them? And stuck up assholes who populate hamlets. "She says you pity me. You stick around because you want to be the gallant knight. That you'll go back to her soon enough."

He could have denied the accusations. He curled his fingers around my ankle and I wrenched my leg away. "I want this to work between us," he said. "I need you to trust me. Tracy is hard work, but she's fragile." He took a breath. "She lost a baby. Our baby."

My heart stopped. His eyes glistened and I couldn't breathe. I buried my head in my arms to block out the sight of him. "Please go."

"Isn't honesty what you wanted?"

I wanted air. I wanted to be sick. I wanted to kick him in the face. "What about Gareth?"

"What about him? He's the kind of guy who loves once, till death and all that crap."

I raised my head. "And yet you'd take away the one thing he loves more than anything."

"She's capable of her own decisions. I didn't do this by myself."

His attitude gave me the shits. "We're done, Ben. I

can't compete with her."

"I don't expect you to compete. I choose to be with you." He scratched his head. "Now you know everything about me. How about you? What's your dark secret?"

Let's sidestep the issue and make it all about me. "I thought you were au fait with all the sordid details."

He laughed. Not a warm funny laugh, but the kind which scrapes the top layer off your heart. "Well then, disprove the gossip mongers, why don't you?"

"How can I defend myself when I don't know what they're saying?"

"You're full of shit," he said.

I walloped him with the pillow and shoved him until he slid off the bed, then my murderous assault ended in a dash for the toilet. He perched on the bath's edge and waited whilst I retched and wailed. "I suppose Tracy doesn't vomit all over the place."

"No. She knows how to behave herself."

Red flag. I hurled myself at him and punched him. He toppled into the bath and took me with him. We scrambled and wrestled and I puked over both of us. Ben forced my arms into a pretzel, and lobbed me out and onto the floor.

"You're insane." He tugged his shirt over his head and wiped his face. "That's one thing they've got right about you."

"Who's right about me?" My muscles went slack from shock. He turned his back on me and washed his face. "Tell me. Who?" Tears stung.

He wrenched a small box from his trouser pocket and dropped it in my lap. "Merry Christmas, Veronica. Or is it Ruth?"

I sat for a long while after he left with the box cupped in my hands. I crawled to bed and sat staring at the wrapping until the sun rose, bright with Christmas joy. My first solo Christmas. Alone. The way I'd intended. Graeme and his horde would spend the day with my mother. No doubt I'd be the hot topic. Ben and the gang would do their thing, without me.

I turned on my phone. A WhatsApp message pinged from Shelly. "Merry Crimbo. Miss you like mad xxx." Two missed calls, a voicemail and a text from my mother. "Call me back."

I slid under the covers, curled on my side and cradled the box against my sore heart.

CHAPTER 17

OBLIVION AND NIHILITY. I'd lost concept of time. The fridge became my enemy, the kettle my salvation. I took stock of one egg, a slither of margarine, enough to coat a corn flake, and a withered red chili. I had herbal tea, cup-a-soup, spaghetti hoops and cereal, sans milk since I'd consumed the last of the long-life.

When I contemplated the front door and the world which lay beyond, panic flared. I perched on the sofa and stared out of the window at the sullen sky. I couldn't remember why I'd come downstairs. I made a cup of chamomile tea and took it to bed.

Using my thumb, I calculated the days on my knuckles, then stared at my hand as if the answers I sought lay in its striations. Months, not days. Dad had taught me to count the number of days in a month. Knuckles for thirty-one days, depressions for anything less.

"*Roo . . .*"

Mum? "Mum?" I ran down the stairs to the front door. I pressed my ear against the wood and listened. A lorry rumbled past. Bin day? I touched my knuckles. Christmas Eve. Christmas Day. Boxing Day. What day came next?

"*Roo . . .*"

"Mum? Where are you?" I dashed to the kitchen door and faced myself in the glass. No, not myself. A gaunt featureless face, framed by lanky hair, shoulders slouched. The eyes lifted and the mouth opened.

I cupped my hands over my ears to block out the screaming. I leapt up the stairs and locked myself in the bathroom. My heart pounded and for the first time in however many days my blood pumped hard enough to clear the fuddle in my head.

The house fell silent. I strained to listen for any sounds beyond the door. Vincent had been gone for . . . my fingers brushed over my knuckles. Not Vincent. "Vincent's gone." My fractured voice resonated off the tiles and startled me. I unlocked the door and tiptoed to my bedroom. Ben's gift box lay unopened on my nightstand. I sat on the bed.

My Christmas Eve dress lay bundled in a corner with a heel poking out the heap. The shoe's twin lay by the wardrobe. I wore an old pair of shorts and a t-shirt stained with God knows what. I'd lost time but couldn't fathom how. I tugged the charger cable and unplugged my phone. The screen lit. Thursday 2 January, 10:41. Nine days? New Year's had come and gone.

I looked out of the window. Shelly's tree lay on the drive. Frost coated my car. The church stood empty, its doors shut, God and Father Murphy on vacation. No one had come for me.

I showered, changed my bedding and put on a load of washing, then wrapped up against the cold and took a walk through the woods to clear the cobwebs out of my head. And to make sure I hadn't been dreaming.

The frozen ground crunched underfoot, and my breath spewed plumes. At the sight of Vincent's tie my spine tingled and my knees trembled. The smell of damp earth and rot conjured thoughts of Ben. And Tracy. I abandoned my walk and fled.

I defrosted my car and drove to town for supplies. I parked at the beach and searched the empty horizon for life's answers. Sky and sea had little to offer other than a brisk and icy wind. I selected Shelly's number from my contacts.

"I'm not speaking to you."

"How're you doing?"

"You could have replied to my messages."

I chewed a fingernail. "Sorry, things got a bit much and I forgot."

"You sound croaky. How's the gang?"

I swivelled in my seat and stretched my legs across the passenger seat. "I don't know. I haven't seen them for a while."

Queue theatrical intake of breath. "Tell me

everything."

"There's nothing to tell. I fell out with Ben on Christmas Eve and no one's spoken to me since."

"Fuckers."

"It's my own fault. It's good to hear your voice." I pressed the phone to my ear, as if the pressure could transfer through the device and connect us.

"Same. I miss your skinny ass."

Tears dripped off my chin. "When are you coming home?"

Dan mumbled in the background. "Dan says hello."

"Hi."

"She says hi. We're driving down on Sunday. I've taken the weekend as unpaid leave because I've used all my holidays."

"I'll see you then."

"You sound weird. Don't let those bitches get to you. And as for Ben, there's plenty fish in the sea, bigger and better ones than him. Love you. See you Sunday." She disconnected.

I dozed, and when I woke a parking attendant stood taking photos of a ticket stuck to my windscreen. Stupid shit could have knocked on the window and told me to move. I opened the window. "Thanks for that."

He pointed to the machine. "Should have paid for a ticket, it's not a campsite."

Streetlights flickered on by the time I got home. I unpacked the car and made a proper cup of tea. I turned on the television and the door knocker clattered.

Felicity stood on the step. "Can I come in?"

"I'm a bit busy."

Her mouth twitched. "It can't wait."

Nine days too late.

She wedged her boot in the gap so I couldn't close the door. "I saw you crawl out your hole, so time for a chat."

"Why now? You've had more than a week to come and see me."

Her eyebrows lifted. "I've been around a few times, Veronica. You've seen me come and go."

"You're lying. Not one of you has bothered to come around."

Felicity took advantage of my hesitation and pushed past me.

"Get out." I caught her elbow and she resisted. "I've got nothing to say to you, or anyone else for that matter."

She spun on her heel. "Look at yourself. What the hell's going on with you?"

"Nothing's going on. What do you want from me? I've got my own life and a job to do. I don't have to have my head up everyone's ass day in and day out."

"Come with me." Felicity stomped to the guest toilet and hit the light switch. She pointed to the mirror. "Take a look at yourself."

I took several unsteady steps and gripped the back of a dining chair. From where I stood I could see the reflection, the face. The eyes caught mine and the mouth extended into a scream.

Felicity's expression registered alarm. She edged past me, her back to the wall. She never once took her eyes off me, and when I turned to follow her she bolted out the door. The screaming wouldn't stop. I blocked my ears and cowered between the sofa and the wall with my eyes squeezed tight.

"Wake up, dozy." Shelly flopped on the bed. "I thought you'd at least have cooked me dinner."

"You're home early." My throat burned. I reached for my water bottle. "I thought you were coming on Sunday."

A frown furrowed her eyebrows. "It is Sunday. What are you on, man?"

"Friday."

"No. It's six thirty, Sunday. I told you I'd be home today." She placed a hand on my forehead. "You're feverish, babe."

"Yeah. I think I've got a bug. Sorry." I rolled away from her and pulled the covers over my head. "I'm glad you're back."

"I'm going to change and then I'll make us something to eat. You fancy anything?"

"Make for yourself. I'm not hungry."

I dozed, and awoke in the woods. Dappled sunlight lit the path. The trees flourished, heavy with leaves, until I reached the rag tree. Not a single leaf adorned the branches. Fireflies swarmed around Vincent's tie, and when I turned, a woman stood at the wood's edge watching me. I recognised her, a familiar stoop to her shoulders, ropey hair. Her lips parted. . .

"Veronica?"

I screeched and tumbled off the bed. Ben dashed around, caught me and lifted me onto the mattress. I flailed with the covers and scooted out of his reach. He hadn't shaved, and bruised shadows lurked beneath his eyes. "What are you doing here?"

"I took a chance that Sean would let me in."

"So you're a big deal because she's back and now you want to pretend you care about me."

He ran his fingers through his hair. "You locked everyone out. I couldn't even get in the kitchen door."

I glanced at the box on my nightstand. I should have hid it. "I might have been lying dead inside."

"You weren't. You watched from the windows, and you know damn well how many times I've been round to see you."

I shook my head. "You walked out on me. Dropped your bombshell and pissed off to gloat."

He sat and placed a hand on my knee. "I did not walk out on you. You locked me out and you said some nasty things." He loosened his grip and leaned across me. "I'm sorry for what I said. I wanted you to know everything so you could trust me." He smoothed away my tears and stroked my cheek with his rough fingers. "I didn't mean to hurt you."

A hollow ache settled in my chest and I sank into my pillows and closed my eyes. "I'm so tired."

The back door swung open and Vincent stood in a sunbeam. He wore his tie and held a scarf in his outstretched hand. I reached for the scarf.

"Coffee for the patient?"

The smell turned my stomach and I slid beneath the covers. "Just water, please Shelly."

"You need to put something in your stomach, babe. You haven't eaten for a week. Your skinny ass is now a bony ass."

I lifted the scarf and the silk furled in the breeze. My nail caught in a frayed corner. I knew this scarf. I looked to Vincent, but the woman from the woods stood in his place. She opened her mouth.

"Ah, shit." Shelly fumbled in the dark. "I've busted my toe on your bed." The bedside lamp flicked on and she loomed over me in swathes of pink satin. "You had a nightmare."

She handed me a glass of water and I swallowed a couple of paracetamols. "My throat's so sore."

"Because you keep yelling and scaring the shit out of everyone." She took the glass. "Babe, if you don't start eating and pulling yourself around you're going to end up in hospital."

"Where's Ben?"

"He's gone home for a shower and change of clothes. Filly's downstairs."

"Tell her to go away."

"She's worried about you. We all are. Elaine popped in for a bit too."

"Tracy?"

"Don't even think about her."

My voice cracked and I sobbed into my pillow. "I can't get her out of my head." Tracy and her baby occupied my every waking thought. And Ben with his arms around them, his family. "I don't know how to stay in this place anymore."

Shelly crouched and took hold of my hand. Her thumb circled the inside of my wrist. "Go back to sleep. I'll be right here."

The woods fell silent and a cloud passed across the sun. They stood at the back door, Vincent, and the woman with a child on her hip. He kissed her hand and her attention shifted to me. Her voice whispered in my ear, laced with hatred and menace. "Bear witness to what I lost, to what you will never have."

Chapter 18

"Sundowners," Shelly said. She placed a tray on the bed with a balletic flourish and poured an orange potion into three tumblers from a vase I'd got as a wedding gift. She passed me a glass, handed one to Elaine, and lifted hers in a toast. "Bottoms up, bitches."

Elaine winked at me and sipped the froth off the top of her cocktail. "We should do this more often. Margaritas between the sheets."

They laughed and we clinked glasses. "Thanks," I said. "I've been a bit morose." Their eyes gleamed with agitation.

Shelly poked a finger in her drink and sucked off the syrup. "You need something with a kick to restart your heart."

"It's nice to see you a bit perkier," Elaine said. "You've had us all worried sick these past couple of weeks."

The front door opened and closed, and someone moved about downstairs. Both became antsy. I clenched my teeth. I had no stomach for whatever game they played. Shelly did a stage cough. Elaine straightened and pressed her lips into a bloodless line. "Veronica, you have a visitor."

Shelly knocked back her drink. "And just so you know, I had nothing to do with this."

Familiar perfume invaded my senses before my mind engaged. I twisted in the bed and looked into my mother's face. "Mum?"

Rachel slid out of her coat, sucked in her cheeks and puckered her lips. "Roo, before you start performing. . ."

"Performing? What are you doing here?" I glanced at Shelly and Elaine. "What have you done?"

"Thanks Lainey," Rachel said. "You two run along." To Shelly, "Take the tray with you. Any chance of a gin and tonic?"

I gave Elaine a death look as she shut the door. I got to my feet and leaned against the wall to steady myself. "How did they find you?"

"Relax darling," she said. "No use getting tetchy with everyone. If you hadn't been so bloody pedantic about this move to start off with you wouldn't be standing here looking at me like I'm something the cat dragged in." She fumbled with her Vape. "You always have to make a bloody scene."

"Don't you dare smoke that in here," I said. "Did

Elaine contact you?"

"Does it matter, Roo? I'm here now."

"Stop calling me Roo. Just stop."

"Jeezus, don't shout. You're giving me a headache." She reclined against the windowsill and sucked so hard on the contraption her neck veins bulged.

"Who called you?"

"Oh calm down. It doesn't matter who called me. The way you're behaving you'd swear I'm some kind of monster." She released a raspberry flavoured steam engine plume and my stomach roiled.

"You are a monster. You and those . . ." I stabbed the air with my index finger, ". . . women, stupid interfering women. This is my house and my life."

"Get dressed and let's get you downstairs. You'll feel better once your blood is moving. Lying in here's not doing you any good." She tilted her chin and twisted her mouth at the state of my bedroom. "This place smells disgusting." She crooked a finger and pressed the end of her nose. "Let's go, baby doll."

"I can't. I need to shower, and I don't think I'll make the stairs."

She boosted herself off the windowsill and dropped the Vape in her bag. "Suit yourself. Whilst you're titivating, I'm going to get my bags offloaded at the bed and breakfast and find out what kind of hole I'm to sleep in."

I had no energy to argue. I knelt on the bed and flopped onto my belly. "What B&B?"

Shelly hovered at the door, and Rachel stepped out the room to claim her gin and tonic. "What happened up there?" she said.

Shelly sounded like a museum tour guide. "Storm damage repairs. A tree fell on the roof and damaged the ceiling. It's fixed now, just needs a lick of paint. Come, I'll show you what's left of the tree, you can see it from my bedroom window."

They wittered on like a pair of hens, and I dozed.

Rachel stuck her head through the doorway. "I'll admit you've inherited my good taste. I could recommend a first-class landscaper for your yard."

"I don't need a landscaper," I said. "And I don't need you."

She gave a mirthless laugh. "You need to catch a wake up, Roo. Everyone's talking about you, laughing at you."

I arranged my pillows and propped myself against the headboard "Really? And you know that how?"

She knelt on the bed, gripped my elbow and whispered through clenched teeth. "They don't give a toss about you. Your ridiculous little friend's been going through your stuff, making fun of you behind your back. How do you suppose I got to hear about all this?"

"Shelly wouldn't do that to me." Her words cut deep. I shrugged out of her grip. "Get out of my house."

"We'll talk about this in the morning, when she's not here." She mimed flappy ears, "Walls have ears."

The church bell clanged once, on the quarter hour. Shelly's snores permeated the walls. I lay on my back surrounded by florets of soggy tissues and watched branch shadows sway across the ceiling. My phone vibrated and the screen lit, casting a white halo. Ben.

"I was going to throw stones at your window," he said.

"Where are you?"

"Parked at the kerb. I would have come round earlier but I heard about Dragon Lady's arrival."

"She's not staying here. I'll throw my keys down." I scrounged for my bag and fished out my house keys. Ben stood beneath my window and caught the bunch. I gathered tissues, did a quick tidy and sprayed perfume, and then got back beneath the covers.

He shut the bedroom door, undressed, and slid his frozen body in next to me. His mouth cut off my squeals. "You're so warm. And you smell great." His arms went around me and his icy hands cupped my buttocks.

The bed creaked and I hushed him. "You'll wake Shelly." He ran his mouth along the curve of my neck and down. Cold hands explored whilst his teeth and tongue teased a nipple, and then I didn't care if he woke the entire southwest coast.

A reticent dawn lurked beyond the window. My bedroom door swung open and my mother faltered, sploshing coffee on the carpet. I adjusted the duvet to cover Ben's naked butt. "Didn't grandma teach you to knock?"

She placed the mug on my nightstand and eyeballed Ben. "You're Eleanor's boy. Benjamin, right?" Ben blanched and managed to reach a seated position without compromising both our dignities. We sat like chastened teenagers. "And this thing you two have going on, whatever you want to call it," she waggled her fingers at us, "you think it's worth the hassle?"

I snagged my t-shirt with a toe. "Get out mum, you're being vile."

"I'll see you both downstairs." She stalked off and left the door ajar. Ben made a dash for his undies whilst I tugged my t-shirt over my head. Shelly snuck past on her way to the bathroom, stuck her finger in her mouth and mimicked a puke.

We showered and dressed, and I perched on the bed. Ben traced his fingertip over the flesh beneath my eyes and kissed my nose. "You don't look so good. You don't have to do as she says, you know. Crawl into bed and I'll bring you some breakfast."

"Can I ask you something?" I scrounged around the bottom of my handbag for his gift box, "Can you give this to me again?"

He smiled. "I want that back, the use-by date expired." He sat next to me and I straddled him.

"I'm sorry for being a bitch. Please give it again."

He handed me the box and I peeled off the paper

and lifted the lid. On a velvet cushion lay an antique gold pendant with an orange stone which caught the light. "It's a fire stone. Opal," he said. I lifted my hair and he fastened the clasp.

The smooth stone felt cool beneath my thumb. "It's beautiful, thank you."

He kissed me. "Walk or carry?"

I slid my feet into my slippers. "I'll walk. You might get side tracked and drop me."

Rachel sat at the dining table and sipped coffee. She tapped a nail on the glass top as she watched us descend. Ben towed me into the kitchen and filled the kettle. We made coffee and toast and joined her. She eyed us, a tactic she'd used on me forever, her silence intended to unnerve. "I'm taking you home," she said.

Ben glanced at me and raised his eyebrows. "How old did you say you were?"

She reached across and placed a hand over mine. "I've managed to get you a referral to the mental health team."

I snatched my hand away and choked on my toast. Her gaze shifted to Ben. "This is not the first time she's gone off tilt. She's prone to these psychotic breaks and things get messy around her. Do you want to saddle yourself with a lunatic?"

"Mum." I shoved the chair backwards and stood. "What are you saying?"

She didn't miss a beat. "You're confused and you're

hearing voices. You can't string a sensible sentence together and you're in a constant state of mania."

"Who told you this?"

"Look at yourself, darling." Her mouth twisted with self-satisfaction. "I don't need anyone to tell me anything. I can see it for myself.

Ben got up and stood behind me. His hands circled my waist. "I think you're forgetting whose house this is," he said. "And it's got nothing to do with you who I saddle myself with."

Rachel rose to the challenge. "How long do you think she can maintain this new life of hers? She can't look after herself, for God's sake. You don't know a single thing about her, about anything. So yes, it has everything to do with me."

Shelly thumped down the stairs in her heels and leaned on the banister. "Sorry to interrupt, I'm off to work babe, see you later."

"Why not stick around," Rachel said. "You're a part of this hullabaloo."

Shelly's chewing gum travelled in slow circles around her mouth. "No, I'm just the lodger."

"Funny coincidence, don't you think? Have you shared with Ruth the small fact that your father and my late husband are brothers?" She peaked her eyebrows and held up her hand to silence Shelly. "And Ben, as it happens your mother is their cousin." She sneered. "All one happy family."

The room spun and my legs went to jelly. Ben held on to me. "Who told you where to find Veronica?"

"What's this Veronica shit?" Swift change of subject. "You think using your middle name changes who you are, makes the slightest difference to how life's going to turn out for you if you stick around here?"

"You've got a real problem, lady." Shelly tugged on her coat and slapped a lipstick kiss on my cheek. "Love you, cuzz."

Rachel's laugh cracked like a whip. "You stupid little prick. I'm here because of your loose tongue."

Shelly's spine stiffened and she turned to me, eyes wide. "Not true. I promise, I did not call her."

"My brother called me." Rachel folded her arms across her chest, eyes on Ben. "It seems his wife and Sean, Shelly, whatever, have a little spy game going on."

Shelly's eyes filled with tears and her bottom lip twitched. She shook her head and followed me to the sofa. My life crashed around me like a broken wave. I had no tears left and my heart sat like a lump of wax in my chest. I clutched the pendant at my throat and wished I could rewind and start again.

"Who's your brother?" Ben and my mother circled one another like cats.

"Gareth." She grinned. "See, I know all about your dirty secrets Benjamin."

Something inside me snapped. I lunged for my mother and smacked her across the face before Ben could catch me. She tottered sideways and dropped to her knees. I struggled in his arms and retched on the stench of burnt toast and sulphur.

"Get Gareth." Ben shouted, and Shelly disappeared.

A whirlwind of sparks wafted up from the floor, circled us and ignited into flames. My flesh seared and beads of sweat coated my face and arms. I tore at my shirt, and at Ben's arms, and all around us an impossible fire wind raged and shrieked. The burning cyclone ejected Ben. He crawled away from me and crouched next to my mother, his body a shield against the flames.

The raging wind enclosed me, obfuscating all sound and vision. With me in the maelstrom's core stood Vincent's woman, eyes ablaze, mouth gaped in a perpetual scream.

CHAPTER 19

I SAT, LEGS CROSSED, and ran my fingers over the scorched and blistered wood where the fire wind had seared a feathered circle into the floor boards. Neither flame nor soot marred the ceiling and walls, and no smell lingered.

Shelly huddled in the Papasan chair. Gareth comforted my mother on the sofa. A red welt marked her cheek and she mopped tears with toilet paper. Ben paced between the kitchen and the lounge and paused every couple of circuits to stroke my hair. Several times he squatted and examined the floor. Once, he leaned forward, touched my chin and looked into my eyes, like he'd catch a clue there to what he'd witnessed.

I had no explanation. He hadn't seen the woman. But then he hadn't seen Vincent either, not until his final moment. Unlike Vincent, she hadn't been a vaporous apparition. She'd stood before me, substantial, static in her hair, her eyes black with hatred and torment.

I turned my palms up and stared at my blistered flesh. How had I been so wrong about Vincent? I'd never once seen him inside the house. Every encounter with him had been serene, and external, intrinsic to the path and the rag tree. None of the violence and horror within had been him.

Gareth got off the sofa and repositioned himself at the dining table. He sat, shoulders hunched, hands clasped between his knees, and glowered at the scorched boards. "How many times do you want me to say you can't stay here? If you do, something terrible will happen."

I looked at him, the sad man with the brooding face, so like my mother's yet I hadn't seen the resemblance. "Why me? Why now?"

He glanced at Rachel, and then his and Ben's eyes met and held. "If you'd have listened to Filly and stopped her buying the house none of us would be sitting here."

Ben scratched his head and resumed pacing. "I tried to stop the sale but the paperwork had gone through. I hoped you'd all be wrong."

"After everything that's happened?" Gareth voice rose an octave. "Rachel, Felicity, and then Tracy. How did you figure we'd all be wrong?"

"I spent the most time here and nothing happened to me." Ben dragged his fingers through his hair. "Something was off, but it's just stuff. One day you feel fine, the next you want to run for the hills. Atmosphere."

Gareth shook his head, mouth pinched and jaw firm. "And you reckon the atmosphere cost the lives of our babies?"

I got to my feet. "In case you two hadn't noticed, I'm right here. What are you talking about?"

Shelly dropped her chin to her chest. Ben rubbed his eyes. Gareth splayed his arms in exasperation. "Why won't anyone come straight with this girl?"

Rachel lifted her face out of her tissue nest. "She won't listen. Thinks she knows everything. You're wasting your time."

I rounded on her. "How can I listen if nobody tells me anything?"

"And she's off screeching again," she said.

Every muscle in my body resisted the urge to give her another smack. "Please, Gareth, cut the drama and tell me what's going on," I glared at Ben, "since nobody else wants to."

"Rach, do you want to tell her?" Gareth said.

My mother shook her head and blew her nose.

He wrung his hands and shrugged. "This site has always had a reputation. As kids we'd take dares to come here at night. Mostly nothing happened, but the summer Rachel and your dad got hitched a bunch of us camped in the ruins after the reception because the guests had taken all the accommodation.

"Camping was Rachel's idea. I'd just turned thirteen. We had Filly with us, she was five. Ben had been born a few months before, so we took her with us to give Aunt Ellie a break. We borrowed a massive tent and a whole bunch of us set up camp."

Rachel lifted her head and sniffed. "Our last bit of childish fun before we settled into marriage."

"Your dad and Bill were trollied," Gareth said. "They fell asleep in the tent and the rest of us sat around the fire telling ghost stories. His gaze slid to the burnt circle. "We almost lost control of the fire a couple of times that night."

My parents' photos resided in a memory box in their attic. I'd often hidden from my mother there, and spent hours sifting through a lifetime of old photographs, and sleeves of overexposed prints, including those taken at their wedding. Gareth, the blue tent adorned with streamers and tin cans, the church, the pub and streets, and the ruin, my ruin, they'd all lived in that box in my secret world.

"Rachel went scrounging for more wood," he said, "and when she stepped back into the ruin she fell."

"I didn't fall. Someone shoved me from behind," Rachel said.

"Rach started to bleed in the night and woke me to go for help. Byron's parents rushed her to hospital."

Rachel plucked at the tissue ends. "I lost my baby."

Shock trickled through me like ice water. She'd never told me about a baby.

"I came back," she said, "a couple of months later. I felt so guilty, and needed Byron to believe me about what had happened. He thought it would do me good to get the trauma out of my system. So we camped under the stars and he made a small bonfire. I awoke in the night to Byron's screams. His sleeping bag had caught alight and he couldn't get the zipper undone." She took several deep breaths. "She. . ." Rachel pointed at the scorched floor, ". . . stood over him and watched him burn."

Shelly shuddered and twisted a curl around her finger. Her eyes travelled from Rachel to Gareth and then to me and she raised her eyebrows.

"I tempted fate and almost got your father killed," Rachel said.

One summer we'd gone to the beach and my dad had stripped to his shorts. I'd never seen him shirtless before and wondered why his skin looked different to everyone else's, mottled and wealed, like melted wax.

Rachel sighed. "He spent the best part of a year recovering from his burns. But the scars never went away, his or mine. We couldn't stay here. He took a job up north and we never returned."

Shelly leaned forward and tilted her head to the side. "What made you come here, babe?"

I turned so I didn't have to look at my mother's face. "He always talked about home. He told me stories about the adventures he and his brother had. His voice carried so much love and sorrow, and when he died, I promised I'd come home for him one day." I scuffed my shoe over the scorched wood. "I wanted to be where his heart belonged."

"You idiot." Rachel flung the tissues onto the coffee table. "Stupid bloody fool."

I sank into the chair next to Shelly. "You couldn't stand that he loved me. You despised every moment he spent with me and not you."

Her laugh cracked like a whip. "Keep telling yourself that, Roo. You were an insipid clingy little shit. You sucked in every ounce of his adoration and left nothing for anyone else."

My childhood memories were like smashed tiles, shards embedded in my soul. Snapshots of my father, always laughing with me. My mother slapping and pinching me for small transgressions, scorn and insults whispered through her clenched teeth.

"I need to go," Shelly extracted herself from the chair and gathered herself into her jacket. "If I'm late again I'll get the sack." Gareth held the door open and Shelly blew me a kiss. "See you later, alligator." She flicked a glare at Rachel and left.

Ben took her place next to me and reached for my hand. "I want to say sorry, but I can see you're full of hell. We need to talk, but not here."

"I'm taking Rach to the house," Gareth said. "You're welcome to come around later once everyone's had time to cool down."

I had no intention of setting foot in Tracy's home, and for all his gallant effort at being the peacekeeper, spineless

Gareth could crawl up his own ass for all I cared. Ben let them out, shut the door, and stood at the scorched circle's centre and contemplated.

"You knew all this but didn't tell me?" I said. "More secrets. One thing after another."

He plunged his hands into his pockets. "Felicity swore me and everyone else to secrecy. She'd convinced herself you had an agenda, and we had no choice but to go along with her."

"Rubbish." I launched myself out the chair and faced him. "You're not a child, Ben. All this pretence of not knowing what's going on, not knowing who I am. So, all this relationship hogwash is part of Felicity's game too?"

"No. The first day I came here, and saw you, I knew my life could never be the same again. You became my future, Veronica. I know that sounds dumb, but it's the truth."

I itched to throttle Felicity, and next time I saw Tracy I'd rip the smirk from her face. What was Tracy anyway? My aunt? Shit. "I need space." I lifted my coat off the hook and let myself out the back. I took Vincent's path through the woods, vented fury on low branches and overgrown bushes, and kicked stones like a sulky child. When the tree came into view, I stopped to catch my breath and sat on a moss draped stump in the silence. No birds sang around the wretched tree. I inhaled the woody blend of damp and rotting mulch and a tinge of smoke from a nearby wood stove.

Twigs snapped on the path behind me. "Benjie said I might find you here."

My hackles rose. Tom rounded the stump and leaned against a tree. I focused on the restless rags whilst my blood cooled.

"I got a call from Gareth," he said. "Seems there's been a bit of bother."

Bother?

"You know if you'd have listened to Gareth things wouldn't have come to this. You've dragged us all into an impossible situation."

I took in the bulk of him, the great big wimp. "What do you want, Tom?"

"You need to finish with Ben, let go of him. All this would never have happened if you hadn't got involved." He coughed breath plumes into his gloved fists. "The minute you and he became a thing Filly went into hyper mode."

I laughed. "Who made her the boss of everything? Who does she think she is?"

"She was there, you know, the night the thing attacked your mother. Just a little girl, but the memory stuck with her always. Rachel didn't see what hit her, but my Filly did and it scared the hell out of her."

"What's that got to do with me and Ben? And why are you the messenger? Where's she? Why can't she face me after she's fucked up my life?"

He folded his arms across his chest and rubbed his

arms. "She's looking out for him. In her mind he's still her baby brother. There's stuff about this place you don't know. Horrible things have happened over the years. Benjie should never have taken the job to rebuild the house but he doesn't see things, you know."

A gust unsettled the branches and the woods creaked. Rags flapped and snapped and dead bracken whispered around us.

"All the time she pretended to be a friend she could have said something, let on she knew who I was, explained things to me. Instead she's gone behind my back and sabotaged my life. She's the cause of all this, not me."

He shook his head. "She hoped you'd be scared enough to leave before things went too far. But you're a stubborn one for sure. I don't know a single person on this earth who'd endure what you have and carry on living in that place."

I got to my feet and swallowed a wave of nausea. "Tell her to grow a spine and come and see me herself. Otherwise fuck off and leave me alone."

CHAPTER 20

I LOCKED THEM OUT, latched the doors, and left a suitcase of belongings on the bottom step for Shelly. My phone buzzed with missed calls and voicemails. Ben knocked several times, first at the front door, then took his chances at the back, though since Vincent's departure the door behaved and denied him access.

I cleaned the house and fretted whilst I worked. Shelly's laundry bag overflowed so I put on a load of washing, cold comfort for throwing her out. She deserved to stew for a bit, and I needed space to think. I couldn't settle and paced the hallway. My phone vibrated and Ben's image flashed on the screen. I let the call go to voicemail, selected Felicity's number and held the phone to my ear.

"Hello?"

Stupid bitch had got Tom to answer. "I want to speak to Felicity." The sound muffled and a whispered argument broke out. Fury heated my already hot cheeks and beads of perspiration coated my top lip. "Tom, give her the bloody phone." The line went silent. I checked if he'd cut me off.

"What?"

"We need to talk," I said, "Just you and me."

Felicity sniffed. "I really can't be bothered with you."

"I don't care what you think of me," I said. "I need to speak to you about what's going on in my house, and what's going on with you. Please, come and talk to me."

"I'm not coming to you. I'll meet you."

"Where and when?"

"At the wood's edge. Half an hour." She cut me off before I could reply.

Wood's edge. Christ. If I owned an axe, I'd chop the fucking tree down.

Twenty minutes later, I sat on a stump and waited. She parked on the opposite side of the road and crossed over. Instead of her grey coat she wore red, like a war flag. I met her halfway, and though I stood almost a foot taller, her attitude made me feel small.

"I have to be somewhere so make it snappy." She stood still as a statue, eyebrows peaked, lips tight.

I raised my arms and dropped them to my sides, defeated. "Tell me what I've done to you so I can at least defend myself." Her expression didn't falter. "Filly, you've got everyone ganging up against me, yet you'll not speak to me yourself."

"You should never have come here," she said. "Worse,

you shouldn't have lied about who you were." She poked a finger at me. "That is what you've done."

I shook my head. "I moved here to make a new life for myself. You were all strangers to me. I came here because my father loved this place and I needed to make my own way in the world, not to deceive anyone. I bought myself a house, made friends, and I fell in love with Ben. I didn't lie about who I am. I had no idea there'd be anyone who'd remember my family. I just didn't want to be Ruth anymore."

She walked past me and stood beneath the misery-infested branches. "Getting involved with Ben was the worst thing you could have done."

"Why? Because of Tracy?"

She faced me, "Yes that, but because of you, who you are, what your family did to mine."

I'd always lacked political finesse. "I don't get where you're going with this. Can you tell me in simple words, forget the ambiguous soap opera revelation?"

"Come here." She walked to the tree and reached into the branches. She nudged the faded blue teddy which swung on its ribbon. "You see this?"

"I know, you lost a baby. Ben told me."

"Did he tell you how?"

"No."

"Once your house's roof went on and he started work on the inside he complained about a constant smell of burning. He asked me to go around, see if I could smell it too. That happened a few times and of course there wasn't anything, just the smell, sickening, like hair burning."

The flesh at the base of my skull tingled.

"Other things happened, tools misplaced, doors opening and closing by themselves. Ben rationalised everything to subsidence, or a breeze. On my grandma's birthday I went to fetch him for a family dinner, and he asked me to take a look around. I went upstairs and everything seemed fine, then on my way down I reached the first landing, and something shoved me from behind. I went over the banister." She gave the teddy another gentle prod and set it off swinging. "I was seven months pregnant. A boy. We got to hold him before they took him. He was perfect."

A lump of sadness constricted my throat. Bolshie Felicity from a moment before hung her head and her shoulders shook as she wept. I took a step towards her and she raised a hand to halt me.

"It took Tracy's baby too, your house."

"Not the house," I said. "You're talking about a pile of bricks and mortar. People take things. And buildings don't push people."

She tugged a tissue from her pocket and blew her nose. "Are you sure you believe that? From what I hear you've been having your own jolly time with your pile of bricks and mortar."

Shelly tattling again. Traitorous twat. "Look, I'm sorry about what happened to you, but it's not my fault.

I didn't come here with an agenda, and I thought we'd become friends."

She composed herself and straightened her collar. "Go home with Rachel. Take yourself back to where you came from." She stepped over the tree's roots and stopped beside me. "We don't want you here. And if Elaine wasn't my best friend, I'd send Bill and Sean packing too."

"And Ben, does he have a say? Or are you the almighty voice."

She snorted. "Ben doesn't have opinions." Her mouth twisted into a sneer. "Haven't you figured him out yet? You're a passing phase. He'll always do as I say, and he and Tracy will always have a connection. They lost a child." Her eyebrows peaked. "That's a bond no one can break."

I followed her to the roadside. "What did my family do to yours? What did you mean when you said that?"

"You're the investigative journalist," she said. "Take a long hard look at your family tree. Speak to your mother and see for yourself."

Standing in the wood's gloom, inhaling its stench of affliction and rot, a vile surge of hatred consumed me. They'd undermined my dreams and my hopes, all of them. Her, my mother, Tracy. I screamed till my voice cracked. Every muscle and vein in my neck and face bulged, rigid and glistening with sweat.

I huddled in bed and slept most of the day. At dusk I surfaced, made a mug of hot chocolate, and upended the boxes containing Dorothy's possessions. I slid the signet ring onto my finger, made the scarf into a bandana, and tied the musty silk around my neck. I unfolded all the letters and reread each one. None provided a clue as to where Dorothy had gone after her meeting with Gladys Hendry. If my property had a reputation, and the entity in my house had caused so much heartache, then wouldn't Dorothy have suffered too, since she'd grown up in the mill and had carried Vincent's baby?

I booted my laptop and scanned my notes from the church registry. According to Father Murphy's account of the mill's history, prior to nineteen thirty-two the property sustained a mundane past. I launched Google, clicked the bookmark for the church's page and opened the aerial image. I zoomed in to the overgrown ruin and traced my finger across the woods to a barren smudge occupied by the rag tree, as if the image and the godforsaken tree held all the answers.

I sifted through the letters and unfolded the undated one.

Dear Mrs Hendry.

I would be grateful if you could come to the mill

for tea. I will be leaving soon and wish to resolve our differences.

Dorothy.

I lay the letter aside and clicked on the burial records icon then selected the surname index. A vein pulsed in my neck and my sweaty fingertips stuck to the keys as I typed. I took a deep breath to calm my nerves and scrolled the archive notes. My hunch paid off. I stared at the screen and a surge of anxiety overwhelmed me.

I got off the bed and bent over to quell the nausea and stop my head spinning. My hands shook as I cradled my phone and dialled Ben. Running to him had become second nature. I cancelled the call. I hooked a finger into the scarf's loose knot and wrenched the thing off my neck.

The burial entry glared on the laptop screen: Killigrew, Dorothy (age 19), Burial date 11th February 1932, Stone 397

My heart raced. I selected the gravestone index and searched for the stone reference. Dorothy's grave lay in plot three, grid reference W5. I opened the churchyard plan and located the plot. The grid reference aligned to an isolated and disorganised cluster of graves. I focused my phone camera on the screen and took a photo.

I returned to the burial records and ran a new index search. I clutched my stomach and gasped as a cramp seized my intestines. Oh God. I snapped the laptop's screen shut and stood. I turned in circles, unable to think. Gladys. The entry stated her name as Hendry-Mackie, buried 15th February 1932. Dorothy and Gladys, buried a few days apart.

I ran to the bathroom and puked clotted hot chocolate. I kneeled and rested my cheek on the cold toilet seat. All the signs had been there, but I'd been blindsided by Vincent. I stood on shaky legs, rinsed my mouth, gulped a handful of water, and returned to my bed.

The curtains fluttered and the voile sheers lifted and bloomed as if floated by a breeze. The air crackled, dry and hot like a kindled fire, and I choked on a waft of rancid fumes. A mesh of black cracks spread from the skirting boards and webbed along the walls like inky watercolour on paper. I got off the bed and backed up until my shoulder touched the door frame. The door handle wouldn't budge in my grip. The curtains fanned and writhed on the airless breeze and the webs thickened to oily arteries and seeped towards me.

"Leave me alone." I shrieked as an immense pressure descended on me and forced me to the floor. Webs fanned into hair-fine threads and invaded my ears and nostrils. Dark strands wove and laced around me and cloaked me in a coarse net. I struggled and choked as the filaments filled my mouth and clogged my throat. I gagged and heaved, and screamed as I tore at my flesh. The room spun. The curtains billowed and snapped.

I twisted beneath the invisible weight and crawled into the narrow gap between the bed and nightstand and clamped my palms over my ears. Hours, or minutes, passed. The stench faded and the crisp cold of predawn settled around me. Moonlight projected branch shadows on the ceiling and walls. My body ached and my teeth chattered.

I felt for the lamp switch and flinched at the light's sudden glare. Blood crusted my legs, arms and fingernails. The wardrobe doors hung open and my clothes lay on the floor. The baby's framed photograph stood propped on the windowsill, and draped over one corner hung my necklace, the fire stone pendant swinging in a gentle arc.

CHAPTER 21

A BLIZZARD RAGED, blotting out the world beyond my arm's reach. I trailed fresh footsteps through the snow, my coat and wellies no match for the squall which shoved me along. The church squatted in a featureless grey gloom and a single light glowed in Father Murphy's office. When I neared the gate, I found his parking spot unoccupied and the church door shut. I sat on the wall, roadside, my feet dangling a foot off the ground. Snow drifted and settled in the ruts of tyre tracks and piled against fences and in corners.

From my perch, my house looked like any other; snow-packed roof, walls pale in the gloom, a benign outer shell for the malign presence resided within. Behind the house the ruin's jagged edges appeared softened by the snow. I could sell, but who would buy the place. Another sad fool like me? I bit my frozen lip and tasted blood.

I tucked my gloved hands under my armpits and attempted to blow plume rings. Beyond the intersection, watery light emanated from the pub, and in the parking lot car shapes huddled beneath a white blanket. I'd alienated everyone. The people I cared about and loved sat less than three hundred yards away but might as well be separated from me by an ocean.

Tyres crunched along the lane and into the church's parking lot. Father Murphy emerge from his car cloaked in a duffle with a tartan scarf wound about his neck like a woollen garrotte. He clapped his leather-clad hands and stomped his boots. "Cold enough for you?"

"I saw the light on and thought I'd wait," I said. I slid off the wall and made my way along the path, careful of hidden ice patches. "I wanted to chat."

He glanced in the pub's direction. "You should be in there. You'll catch your death out here."

I should be so lucky.

He slid a key in the door's lock, leaned a shoulder to the wood and gave the bottom corner a stiff kick. The door shuddered open and a flurry of snow claimed new territory. "Come on in, it's not much warmer here but the office will be toasty."

I trailed him to the office and perched on the radiator with my back to the window casing. He fussed with his layers and sank into his chair. "Chat away."

"I've done a bit of digging," I said. "Put together a family tree and researched the online records like you suggested."

He nodded and pursed his lips.

"You could have saved me a lot of time and heartache if you'd told me everything when I came to you the first time."

"I wanted to, believe me." He peaked his eyebrows. "But you were settling in, finding your feet, and indulging Vincent." He cleared his throat. "You're very young, your maturity belies your age, and in the scheme of things what do the musings of an old man matter? I thought it a passing phase, this research of yours."

Bloody ridiculous. "Why does everyone treat me like I'm an idiot child?" My voice resonated in the office's confines. "And is now a good time for you to tell me?"

He leaned back and clasped his hands in his lap. "I'll tell you what I know, but you should speak to Arthur. I'm seeing him tomorrow. You can come along and get the story from the horse's mouth."

"What happened to Dorothy and Gladys Hendry?"

"The circumstances surrounding their deaths is hearsay, of course," he said, "but the coroner's enquiry ruled both as accidental. House fire. The Killigrews fell on hard times after the war and the mill fell into dilapidation. A firetrap." He opened his drawer and extracted an envelope. "Some old photos and documents you might want to take a look at."

I reached for the envelope and picked at the seal.

"The Mackies once had influence in this area. Big

shots. Bullies. Now they're less than a handful of ordinary folk. Being the wife of a vicar, and a Mackie to boot, put Gladys Hendry in a powerful position. She came from money. That's how she kept her family name. She couldn't inherit her father's estate otherwise."

I slid the photographs out of the envelope and sorted through them. A flush of goosebumps sprang up on my skin and I shuddered.

"Gladys had no intention of letting her eldest son marry a Killigrew. She had a society engagement in mind for him, and the poor boy fled and joined the army. Needless to say he got Dorothy pregnant before he left."

I couldn't tell from the first two monochrome images where my ruin originated. Another shot taken from the structure's rear showed the mill wheel and I recognised the door and windows. The last image showed a dark-haired girl in a sundress sitting in front of the mill.

"Gladys made the poor girl's life unbearable." Father Murphy leaned forward and propped his elbows on the desk. "When Vincent died, she spread vicious rumours to discredit Dorothy, and when the time came, she took the baby. During the two years spanning the baby's birth and her demise, Dorothy, quite understandably, became a troubled soul and spent time in a lunatic asylum."

I clenched my jaw and bit into my cheek.

"They discharged her into her mother's care on twenty-fifth January nineteen thirty-two. The fire happened on February third."

I skimmed the documents. Dorothy's death certificate, and a discharge note from Cornwall County Mental Hospital, citing Dorothy Killigrew's condition as mental anxiety. "What about her mother?"

"No mention of her in the records. She must have moved away after the fire."

I returned the photos and documents to the envelope. "Can I keep these?"

"Yes." He got to his feet and massaged his back. "I'll be going around to Arthur's at eleven in the morning. You're welcome to meet here and we can walk across together."

I slid my hoodie over my head and let myself out. A car crawled into the intersection and manoeuvred a slow turn into the pub's car park. I trudged across the road and reached the doorway at the same time as the car's occupants. Penny's spiteful face peered at me through a muss of psychedelic unicorn fur. She pulled her face into a sneer and shoved herself through the doors.

Her father supported an older woman, her shoulders hunched but eyes sharp, into the pub's sheltered entrance. I stepped aside to let them through, but the woman stopped and tilted her face to look at me.

"You're Rachel's girl?" she said.

"Come on, Gran." The man's hand fastened around the woman's elbow.

She slid her arm from his grip. "Go inside. I'm coming."

He lingered for a moment and she shooed him. "I've

been hoping I'd catch you around," she said. She winked and grinned. "They watch me like a hawk, you know. Like I'm going to make a break for it, or disappear in a puff of smoke or something."

"Hi, I'm Veronica." I extended my hand, which she took and folded in her own.

"Benjie's told me all about you. He's quite smitten." Her smile crinkled her nose. "It's about time too. No man should be mollycoddled by his sister. Mind you, it's not Felicity's fault, she has issues, but the problem is he's let her get away with it far too long."

A shadow darkened the door's mottled glass window. She inclined her head. "They'll be out for me in a second. Do you like the necklace?"

Her question caught me off guard. I lay my hand over the spot on my chest where the pendant should have been.

"I hope you can cherish it like I did. It's all I had of my mother."

The door swung inward and Felicity stood clutching the handle. She glared at me. "Gran, what are you doing out here?"

The woman gave her a limp wave. "Keep your knickers on. I'm chatting to Veronica."

Over Felicity's shoulder I caught sight of Shelly crossing the bar. She blew me a kiss over a pile of dishes and disappeared through the kitchen door. I'd thrown her out and she blew me kisses.

"Come on then," Felicity said, "Your tea is getting

cold."

"Oh all right then. I hope we get to talk some more soon," the woman said, and turned to follow Felicity. "Come to Colette's for tea some time."

The door banged shut and swung open. Ben stepped out and stretched his beanie over his ears. He took in my wellies and grimaced. "You coming in for a beer?"

"No. I was hoping to catch Shelly."

He tugged my scarf ends and pulled me into a hug. "You locked me out. Again."

I clung to him. Inhaled his familiar aftershave and sawdust scent. "I need space. My mother's right. I'm a mess."

"Now I've met her, I can see that she's your problem. She's nasty." He cupped my face. "I don't blame you for trying to get away from her. We need to run her out of town."

I ignored his attempt at humour. "She'll be stuck here for days with this storm." I let go of him and stepped onto the path. "Tucked up all nice and cosy at Tracy's place. Wouldn't you love to be a fly on the wall?"

"Come inside, please," he said.

"No. I'm not wanted here." He didn't contradict me, just tucked his hands in his pockets and stared at his boots. An ache radiated from my heart to my fingertips. "I'm going to see Arthur tomorrow morning. Father Murphy's taking me. I could meet you afterwards for a coffee. Tell Shelly I'll give her a ring later."

He took a step towards me, then changed his mind. "See you tomorrow then."

Arthur Mackie greeted us, cheerful and nimble despite hunched shoulders, and waved us through to his sitting room whilst he proclaimed his achievement at reaching the ripe old age of ninety-seven. We entered a cluttered room, and Ben stood at the window talking to a woman with grey hair twisted into a loose bun.

Agnes Eden, Arthur's carer and companion, introduced herself and indicated for us to sit. Father Murphy took a corner chair, which left me and Ben the couch, a hard-backed olive green number with hundreds of brass rivets decorating the edges of the upholstered backrest and sides. The dark wood gleamed from years of polishing and the cushions, though thinned, held firm when we sat.

Ben lifted the hatbox out of my arms. "What are you doing here?" I said. He placed the hatbox on the floor next to the Queen Anne coffee table, and Agnes took off to the kitchen to set the tea tray.

Arthur flopped into an ancient striped deco chair with sides which resembled oversized wagon wheels. "Eh lad, it's been a while since."

Ben grinned. "A whole week, at least, Uncle Arthur." He placed a hand on my knee and squeezed. "I thought you might like some moral support."

"Liam here's told me all about your mystery," Arthur said. He peered at me over his black-rimmed glasses, the lenses so smudged no wonder he needed to look past them.

"Coo-ee."

Ben heeded Agnes's call, his footsteps extracting painful cracking sounds from the floorboards. He arrived bearing a tray packed with tea paraphernalia, and a plate of crustless triangle sandwiches. Agnes poured the tea and handed cups around.

"What you got, lassie?" Arthur said.

I lifted the box's lid. At the sight of the photographs, Agnes inhaled, clutched her chest, and left the room at such speed the floorboards forgot to squeak.

"Oh now," Arthur said, gripping his hand rests, "there's a blast from the past." He gestured for the photos. "Could that be little Alice? My good grief."

Ben and I hunched forward. Arthur picked out the picture of the seated girl. Agnes returned with a tissue pressed to her nose and dropped into the twin of Arthur's dreadful deco chair. "That's Alice," she said.

"Yes. Married your grandpa," Arthur said, waggling an arthritic finger at Ben.

Ben frowned. "What's her picture doing in there?"

"Lemme see the rest," Arthur said. Ben positioned the box at the old man's feet, and he and Agnes fiddled with the contents. "This is Alice at her confirmation. And this one, taken when she and James Marshall left for their honeymoon, nineteen fifty....what was it, Aggie?"

"First of November, nineteen fifty-two. She was a full moon bride. We called her Mrs Moonshine. She loved the name." Agnes dabbed her nostrils. "My sister Lucy and I were bridesmaids."

"Nineteen fifty-two. 'ell of a debacle about the full moon, I remember," he chuckled. "And this one 'ere is my brother, Vincent." Arthur's voice dipped. "Right ansum boy 'im. Seventeen when 'e snuffed it. Such a bloody waste."

"What happened?" I asked, wary of stirring a hornet's nest.

"Knocked off his scooter by Stanley Benham." Agnes spoke her words as if they tasted bad. "The day he arrived home on army leave."

"Yep, did a thorough job, 'e did," Arthur said. "Wiped the poor soul out. Lad didn't see it coming."

Agnes tutted into her tea.

"And Dorothy Killigrew up the spout," Arthur said. "Did not impress my parents in the least. They waited for 'er to pop and nabbed Alice before she'd had a chance to take 'er first breath."

Ben traced his fingers along my thigh, the motion warm and soothing.

"Poor lass ne'er got over it. A few weeks after the second anniversary of Vincent's passing she topped 'erself."

My cup clattered in its saucer and tea slopped on my legs. Agnes dashed for a cloth. I glanced at Father Murphy. "You said her death was accidental."

"Ruled accidental by the coroner," he said.

"Then how did Dorothy . . ." A lump constricted my throat. Ben placed a hand over mine.

Arthur drummed his fingers on the chair's arms and made a guttural growl. "Bloody awful mess she made of it. The lass lured Mother to the mill, banged 'er over the 'ead, and then 'anged herself."

"Stanley Benham had it in his mind to court the lass," Agnes said.

"She wanted none of it." Arthur thumped the arm rest. "Chucked stuff at 'im every time 'e called on 'er." Arthur paused. "No surprise."

Agnes made a strangled sound. "The day of the fire, Stanley called at the mill to see Dotty."

"Swingin' from the banister," Arthur said, "and Mother lay on the floor, the whole downstairs on fire. 'e shouted around for 'elp, broke the window to get to 'er but the fire 'ad them all. Collapsed the whole place down on their 'eads."

Ben and I sat in muted silence. Agnes gazed into her empty cup. Father Murphy placed his cup on the tray and walked to the window to look out.

"Stanley went cracked after that," Arthur said. "Police got no straight word out of 'im."

Ben burrowed in the box and brought out the tobacco

tin. He popped the lid and pulled out a newspaper cutting, the paper yellowed and flimsy. "That's what this is." he said.

I unfolded the article, trimmed from The Cornishman, March 24th, 1932. A few lines in a column attested Arthur's story of Gladys and Dorothy's fate, and the coroner's ruling of a tragic accident. The truth had been right under my nose all this time.

CHAPTER 22

"YOU NEED TO SEE A DOCTOR, BABE." Shelly crouched next to me, swept her hair over her shoulder, and stroked my back.

"I'm fine. It's just nerves."

"I've got nerves," she said. "You don't see me puking all day."

"That's because you're too busy poncing around annoying people."

She helped me to my feet. "Make an appointment. I'm serious. How long have you been like this?"

"I will. Stop nagging." I washed my face and took the offered towel. "I need to go into Perranporth next week, so I'll do it then."

"Let me know when. I'll come with." She followed me to the bedroom.

"I don't need you to hold my hand," I said.

"News flash, it's not all about you. I've also got things I need to do in town."

I shot a glance at the photo frame on the windowsill hoping she wouldn't notice and start an interrogation. I got into bed and drew the cover over myself. "I'm glad you're back. I missed you."

She paused in the doorway. "At least until you chuck me out again."

Ben's arms circled my waist and his breath warmed my neck. His lips touched my ear and sent a shiver along my spine. "I like it when you get to stay over at mine."

His idea of making up involved dinner at the pub, supermarket flowers, and makeup sex. "At this rate I'm going to need my own shelf space." I dropped my toothbrush into the holder next to his. "And a drawer for my underwear."

He nibbled my earlobe. "You don't need underwear in my house." He lifted my t-shirt over my head and cupped my breasts. "Just naked flesh."

"Ouch." The heat his kisses had ignited cooled.

"Sorry. Did I hurt you?" He softened his grip and his thumbs circled my nipples.

"No. I'm just feeling a bit tender."

He folded me in his arms and kissed my neck. "I'm not surprised. You've had a shitty couple of weeks."

I got into bed and stacked the pillows against the headboard. "I need to talk to you."

He got in next to me and slung an arm across my belly. He trailed kisses along my clavicle and latched on to a nipple whilst his fingers trailed lower and slid into my panties.

"Ben, stop. I'm serious."

He raised his head and frowned. "What's the matter? I thought we were sorted."

A different kind of heat welled up inside me. My heart hammered against my ribs and sweat broke out on my palms and the souls of my feet. "Sit up."

"You need to work on your timing." He shifted, tugged the duvet over himself and crossed his legs.

I cleared my throat and took a deep breath. "I'm pregnant."

His expression froze and his eyes searched mine. A vein pulsed in his neck and a jaw muscle twitched. "How far gone?"

"About six weeks."

His eyes flickered, mental mathematics working out in his head. He stiffened and gripped his knees. "Why did you wait so long to tell me?"

Not the desired reaction. "I didn't know until I went to see the doctor yesterday." A twinge of anxiety twisted my insides. He nodded and stared at his hands. I fidgeted, awkward and self-conscious. "Say something."

"I don't know what to say." He swung his legs off the

bed and kept his back to me.

"Can you at least look at me?"

He stood and put his boxers on. "Get dressed. I need to think."

I stared at my reflection in his mirror, a stranger in a stranger's bedroom. I dressed, gathered my stuff and found him perched on a stool in the kitchen. "Anything you want to say before I go?"

"I can't do this," he said. "I can't go through this again."

"This, again?"

"Tra—"

"Don't dare bring up Tracy." I gripped the doorframe to hold myself steady. "Do not make a comparison between me and her. When you find something you want to say that doesn't involve her, call me." I left by the back door and waited at the garden gate. My breath billowed and tears froze on my cheeks. When he didn't come after me, I diverted through the churchyard and crouched in the doorway. I sobbed into my gloves until I lost my breath, and then cried until I had no tears left.

Felicity was right about the hold Tracy had on Ben. He didn't want me.

Us.

"Oh my God." Shelly's arms shot up, one hand clutching

a letter, the other a torn envelope. She spun on her heels and stomped into the kitchen. "Oh. My. God."

I slugged a couple of painkillers and glared at her over my coffee mug. "What?"

"I'm on the waiting list." She pirouetted. "I'm on. The fucking. Waiting list." She flapped the letter at me. "Surgery."

The coffee seared my throat. "When?"

She dropped her arms and shrugged. "Dunno. Could be months or years."

"How can you plan your life if you don't know when anything's going to happen?"

"I don't care how long I have to wait. I'm on the list and that's all that matters." She twirled and slapped my rump as she sashayed past me.

"Good for you."

She stopped and stood hands on hips. "Who pissed on your parade?"

I gulped the last mouthful of coffee and dropped my mug into the sink. "Sorry. I'm being an ass."

"Yeah you are. And anyway, I thought you were staying over at Ben's."

I leaned against the counter and held out a hand. "Show me the letter."

"No. Don't change the subject. Why didn't you stay over?"

Sharing my secret with Shelly would amount to posting an announcement on Facebook. "Ben and I are finished."

"You two make me giddy." She folded her letter into its envelope and gave me a hard look. "So much drama for such a short romance. But you're young and there's a lot of fish out there."

I added fish intolerance to my mental list of life's woes. "What's your plans for the weekend?"

"I'm on late tonight and then I'm covering for Kenver tomorrow and Sunday. He's taking his missus away for her birthday and wants me to stay over, keep an eye on things. I'll book you a table for dinner tomorrow if you fancy. You can keep me company."

Shelly left for work and I sulked on the sofa and checked work emails. I'd managed to relegate myself from rising star to the soon-to-be-unemployed bracket. I scanned through pleas for articles and veiled threats from my editor following missed deadlines.

I opened my research folder and scribbled names and dates on post-its and arranged them on the wall. By sunset I had a semblance of a diagram mapped out.

At midnight, Shelly and The Beast from the East blew in with a bottle of Sambuca. She stripped to her t-shirt and leggings, piled her jacket and scarf on the Papasan chair, and went for shot glasses. "Light a candle," she said. "You can't drink Sambuca without a flame."

"I'm not drinking, with or without flame."

My words fell on deaf ears. She planted a glass on the table in front of me, took a swig from the bottle, and eyed my diagram. "What's this?"

"Family tree." The smell of alcohol turned my guts.

She winked at me. "You have way too much time on your hands. You need a proper job" She trailed a finger across the post-its and dislodged a few which floated to the floor, "Oops, my bad."

"Leave it." I retrieved the notes and replaced them on the wall.

"How come Dorothy's on your family tree?" She flicked the note with Dorothy's details.

"A discussion for when you're sober," I said. "I'm going to bed." I made a run for the stairs and reached the toilet in the nick of time.

Shelly shouted up. "If I was a betting woman, I'd say you're knocked up, girlfriend."

A silence settled around me. The kind where my mother would say an angel passed through. Except no angels dared set foot in my house. The bathroom door creaked and slammed. Shelly screamed.

"No." I got to my feet and wrenched the door open. A fug of smoke clogged the stairwell and spread along the ceiling, and the lights tripped. "Shelly?" I ran towards the stairs. I gripped the banister, lost my footing, and slid down the first flight on my backside.

I felt my way across the landing and gagged on smoke and the stench of burning hair. "Shelly?" I stood, and a force struck me between the shoulder blades. I sprawled, spread eagled, and landed at the foot of the stairs.

A howl came from the lounge. I felt around the floor to get my bearings and my fingers closed over a small familiar shape. My pendant. I clutched the stone and crawled along the skirting board towards the sound. "Shelly, where are you?"

The Sambuca bottle spewed flames and beads of fire bloomed and spread across the floor. In the glow I spotted her crouched behind the blazing Papasan. I dropped the pendant into my pocket, slid the chair away from her and helped her up. "Get outside." I shoved her to the door, grasped the cushion and the clothing and dragged them out onto the drive.

I ran inside, grabbed the throw off the sofa and smothered the flaming alcohol, then sat, chest heaving, as the cold air permeated my pyjamas. Shelly stood outside shivering, arms wrapped around herself. The cushion had soaked up snow and smouldered in a sooty puddle. "You're a fucking disaster," I yelled.

I reset the trip switch and doused her arms and face with cold water. Flames had singed her hair and blisters bubbled along her arms, lip and hairline. I settled her on the bottom step with a glass of Coke and squeezed in next to her.

"I'm so sorry," she said, "You saved my life."

I lay an arm across her shoulders. She'd suffered more damage than the house. The floor would get away with a sanding and my chair needed a new cushion, but she'd messed up her face and hair and her clothes were ruined.

"You drink too much and you're lethal with candles."

Her head twitched. "I didn't light the candle."

"You must have. The fire didn't start by itself."

"No, babe, I promise you I did not light the candle. I was joking around with you and next thing something smacked me on the head and then everything was on fire. I didn't do this."

A draft behind me prickled the hairs on my neck. "We're a right pair of crazies," I said. I dug in my pocket and brought out the pendant. "Did you take this from my bedroom?"

Shelly touched the stone. "I've never seen this before."

"You have. Ben gave it to me for Christmas. I wore it the day my mother came. I left it on the windowsill in my bedroom."

"I swear to you, I don't remember seeing it. Cross my heart."

"I found it on the floor, right there." I pointed to a spot at the bottom of the stairs.

She shook her head. "Not me. You need to have a word with your spook. She's going to kill us. I don't know why I came back here. This place gives me the screaming shits."

I got Shelly to bed and lost track of time. I showered and crawled into bed five minutes before my alarm went off. I looped the pendant around my neck and fastened the clasp. If I wore the damned thing then it couldn't go walkabout.

"Hey?"

I hugged my pillow and groaned. "Go away."

"What happened? The house stinks of smoke, downstairs is a mess and there's stuff strewn across your driveway?"

"There's a cushion, a coat and a scarf on the driveway, Ben. Nothing is strewn across anywhere." I gave him a fisheye. "Who let you in?"

"I caught Sean. . . Shelly leaving for work."

"How is she?"

"I didn't pay attention. I'll put the kettle on. Get up and come downstairs."

I shuffled into the kitchen and swallowed air to stop myself retching. "What are you cooking?"

"I'm making you an omelette. You're not looking after yourself."

Oh, for the love of God. Now he wanted to mother me. "I can't eat." I ran to the guest loo and hurled.

"Sorry, I didn't think the egg would make you sick. Can I get you anything?"

I shrugged his hand off my shoulder. "Give me space, will you?"

He backed away and hovered in the doorway. "What can I do? Do you want a glass of water? I've boiled the kettle, let me make you a tea."

I kicked the door shut. "Leave me alone. Go to Tracy.

Go to hell for all I care."

"I'll make tea. Don't be long."

Fuck. Shit. Dammit. I kneeled on the cold tiles until my stomach settled. I wiped tears on my sleeves and bit into the wound in my cheek until a warm gush of blood filled my mouth.

CHAPTER 23

BEN'S FORM MOULDED TO MINE, our legs tangled. His breath blew steady cold snuffles between my shoulder blades, interrupted by an occasional snore. I listened for Shelly coming home, but knew she'd stay over at the pub. She'd not spent a night in the house since the fire.

I dozed, and jolted awake. A warmth soaked the bedding beneath me, moist and unpleasant. Lifting Ben's arm, I slid out of bed. A dark stain covered my legs and the sheets. My heart palpitated and fear clenched my gut. I felt for the light switch and blinked in the sudden light.

"What are you doing?" Ben shielded his eyes and raised himself on an elbow.

My body trembled. "Toilet. Sorry about the light." I snapped the lamp off and I slid a hand between my legs. Dry. Just a dream.

"Get in. It's freezing." He rolled onto his side and

faced away from me.

I skimmed a hand across the sheets, got into bed and curled my feet into the curve of his knees. I lacked courage to lie with my back to the door, so lay against Ben and stared into the darkness.

A rush of warm fluid between my thighs woke me. I peeled back the duvet and ran to the bathroom. Nothing happened when I tapped the light switch. Cold seeped from the floor, and the window rattled against the wind. I found the toilet and dropped my pyjama bottoms. A clammy stickiness coated my legs and hands.

My baby.

"Ben?"

The door slammed and a hard blow struck my head. I slumped off the toilet and cowered against the bath, legs tangled in my bottoms. A second blow caught me on my back and winded me. "Ben? Help me."

Icy fingers clawed at my hair and wrenched my shoulders. I crouched with my forehead pressed to the floor and cradled my belly with both hands as blow upon blow struck my head and body. A phantom hand grasped my hair and lifted me almost to my feet, then slammed into my stomach. I collapsed onto the floor and crawled towards the door. "Help me."

Light shattered the darkness and I screamed. The door swung into me and Ben shoved against the wood until I slid out the way and he reached for me. "What the hell are you doing on the floor?"

I kicked him and slapped his hands away from me. "Blood. I'm bleeding."

"Veronica, calm down. There's no blood." He kneeled and helped me dress. "You've had a nightmare. There's no blood." He held me, a hand cradling my head against his chest. "Deep breath. You're not bleeding." His own breath came in ragged gasps.

He settled me in bed and fell straight back to sleep. I lay and watched branch shadows on the walls, and the deeper shadows beyond, the ones which waited. I imagined a future for my child and myself, but couldn't see past this point. My mind drifted, niggled at my post-it family tree. I'd made all the connections, right down to Dorothy and Vincent. All, except one vital link to close the loop.

At last a grey gloom cracked the night and I fell asleep.

"I can't come back." Shelly rocked her chair and ran her fingers through her new style cropped shoulder length hair. "That place is fucked up. I'm too scared to even look at your house."

"A house can't hurt you," I said. "You cause your own drama half the time. You were drunk and it was an accident."

"Why won't you believe me?" She tilted forward and grabbed my hands. "I didn't light the candle."

I knew she hadn't. She'd never brought it from the kitchen and the wick remained fresh, unburnt. "I do believe you. I just don't want this between us."

She pursed her lips, formed a word then thought better of what she had to say. "I love you babes, nothing's between us. I'm doing this for me. Kenver's going to train me to be assistant manager and I get to live in as part of the job."

Convenient. "Fine. But you'll still come and see me?"

Her head twitched a fraction. She touched the blister scabs on her hairline. "No. I'm not ever coming to see you whilst you're in that house." She sipped her beer. "I think you should move in to Ben's whilst you're . . ." She pointed at my belly.

"I can't move in with him." I covered my face with my hands. "I'll forever be in Tracy and Felicity's line of fire. Besides, I don't know if we'll even work out. When I told him about the baby he didn't say a word. He let me walk home in the snow and next day there he was. No apology. No further discussion. I don't know where I stand with him."

"It's safer, just 'til you make up your mind about shit." She scratched her scalp, fluffing her curls and flopping a strand over her singed fringe. "It's a no brainer, house or baby. Personally, I don't think you can have both."

Nothing she said was untrue. "I can't run away from my own house. Imagine what everyone will say."

She stood and collected our empty glasses, "You're a

bigger asshole than I thought. Selfish, just like your mum. You'd risk your baby's life to save face. Good luck with that."

"Don't be nasty. I mean I'll never be able to sell the house," I said.

She smirked. "But you won't try?"

"I am trying." Estate agents had come and gone and sent their valuations. I had papers to sign but found ways of avoiding making a decision. I had everything to lose. My home, my freedom, now my baby. "It's not that straightforward."

She tapped a finger on her temple. "You're nutso. Move in with Ben. Sell the house. Then when your baby comes you can make whatever decisions you need to, with or without him."

I left the pub and crossed the intersection. I needed an exorcist, not a shoulder to cry on. I let myself in, boosted the heating and climbed the stairs. Ben's number rang and I lay on my bed with my phone propped between my shoulder and ear.

"Hey. I'm still in Perranporth." He spoke through a full mouth.

"What are you eating?"

"A sandwich. What's up?"

I recognised a voice in the background humdrum and a bubble of fury burst in my chest. "Who are you with?"

"No one. Just picking up some lunch. I've got the bank at three and then I'll head home. What's your plan for tonight?"

"I've got stuff to do. See you around." I cut him off. Tears slid off my cheeks and pooled in my ears. I rolled myself in the duvet and let fatigue take me.

I lost the day to sleep. A headache pounded behind my eyes and my body refused to budge. I dozed on and off and woke startled when my phone vibrated itself off the nightstand and hit the floor. "What?"

"You need to get me a key cut."

"You can have Shelly's."

"Let me in then." For emphasis he banged on the door.

I opened to a bouquet of guilt flowers.

Ben lowered the bunch and smiled. "Sorry I'm late."

I bit back a choice of nasty remarks and left him on the doorstep.

"Hey, what's the matter?"

"You're the matter." I turned on him. "You think I'm stupid? I know you spent the day with Tracy. I heard her talking in the background when I phoned you."

He dumped the flowers on the kitchen counter and plunged his hands in his pockets. "I bumped into her and your mother and they bought me lunch. I didn't spend the day with her."

"That's all you had to say when I asked. You said you were with no one. You're a fucking liar."

"I didn't want a scene. They were sat looking at me."

"What happens now Ben?" I crossed my arms and

leaned against the banister. "With us. With our baby."

He paced the kitchen. "I don't know. What do you want?"

"Forget what I want. What happens now? Do you want the baby?"

He gave me a dark look and frowned. "Do we have to talk about this now?"

Unbelievable. I blinked hard to fight back tears. "How about now or never."

"That's a bit harsh. You drop this on me and expect a miracle decision."

Blood rushed in my ears and my stomach flipped. "You're right. What was I thinking?" I stomped across the charred floor and wrenched the door open. "Get out of my house. Piss off to Tracy."

He scowled at me. "You've got a serious problem, Veronica. Time you grew up."

My hand connected with his cheek. We glared at one another, both shocked. He zipped his jacket and walked to his van without a backward glance. I shut the door and slid to the floor, buried my head in my arms and wailed until I lost my voice.

CHAPTER 24

COLETTE AND HARRY'S COTTAGE nestled amidst a cluster of lodges surrounded by orchards and fields. I knocked, and moments later the door opened and Penny's face appeared. She gave me and the hatbox cradled in my arms a cursory glance before she stepped aside, bowed and waved an arm in a dramatic arc. "Better come in."

"Veronica." Colette exited the kitchen and confused me with air kisses to both cheeks which resulted in an almost lip kiss. "I'm so pleased you could come."

She led me into an open plan lounge which overlooked a hedged garden, and beyond, the moor. "Gran, look who's here. Veronica, this is Granny Alice."

Alice.

The woman I'd met at the pub during the snowstorm sat huddled in an armchair. She placed a handful of knitting on an occasional table, got to her feet and took my hands in hers. "At last you've come to see us."

"Thanks for the invite. I've never been this far down the track before."

"How's your ghost?" Penny discarded her crocs and lay on the sofa, legs stretched out, arms hooked behind her head.

I placed the hatbox on the floor. "No such thing as ghosts," I said.

"Rubbish." Penny sat and gaped at me. "I saw him with my own eyes."

"I heard he's passed on," Alice said. "Released from whatever kept him here."

"Cool." Penny narrowed her eyes at me. "So, there is such a thing as ghosts."

Defeated by a snotty teenager.

Penny looked past me and out the window. "Don't you get creeped out about what happened in your house?"

Alice clucked her tongue. "Away with you and your silly comments."

Penny glared at Alice. "I'm talking. You can't just chase me away. You're not the boss of me."

Her tone set my teeth on edge. "The house didn't exist before I came along so no, it doesn't creep me out."

"Still, the place is built on the mill site, so awful stuff happened right under your feet." She clamped a hand around her neck, stuck out her tongue and tilted her head to the side.

Colette brought in the tea tray and glared at her.

"Homework, Missy."

Penny slid her feet into her shoes and made a face as she passed me.

Colette waved a hand. "Ignore her, she's a freak."

"Does Felicity know you asked me around?" I couldn't bear the thought of her pitching up and humiliating me.

Colette handed me a cup of tea. "I'll be honest, I tell her as little as possible. Ben might like to live under her thumb, but I prefer a bit of distance between us."

"We get minimal interference out here," Alice said. "It's not healthy living in one another's pockets." She eyed me over her teacup's rim. "If you have any hope of a life with Benjie I suggest moving to Canada."

Colette laughed. "Gran's exaggerating."

Gran had hit the nail square on the head. I took a sip of tea and scanned a series of fox hunt paintings which lined the far wall. An ancient copper bed warmer and a brass barometer occupied the opposite space along with a selection of clocks and horsey bric-a-brac. Colette's furnishings might be contemporary, but everything else in the house belonged to a bygone era.

"Jokes aside," Alice said, "Felicity does tend to complicate things."

I glanced at Colette. She shrugged. "It's the nature of the beast, I'm afraid. You've come along and ruffled her perfect feathers."

On the wall behind her, several small framed paintings dangled from brass hooks, amongst them an identical painting to the one my father had given me as a graduation gift.

Alice followed my gaze and grinned, "Pretty aren't they? The little floral is one of a pair."

I went across and examined the ornate frame which contained a miniature floral centrepiece.

Alice's eyes gleamed. "This stash got divvied between brothers, my James and his brother Frederick. They both had their own families and wanted little from the meagre estate, so they palmed off most of everything but kept all the paintings. The miniatures were a wedding gift from their father to their late mother, my niece Georgina."

My head spun "I have one almost identical to this."

"And so you should," Alice said. "Frederick Marshall is your grandfather."

A wave of nausea turned my stomach.

"Veronica, are you all right?" Colette touched my arm.

"Sorry, I haven't been too well." Less than half an hour and already making an ass of myself. I sat, slugged my tea, and clutched the saucer in my lap. "Did Ben tell you I've been researching my house's history?" I said. "I've been working on a family tree, but the information I've got is patchy based on what I found in the church registers."

"We've heard all about your research," Alice said. She chuckled. "Filly hopes you're on a wild goose chase."

"I get the feeling Ben does too," I said.

Colette eyed the hatbox. "Did you find anything worthwhile in there?"

I placed the cup and saucer on the table and pressed my hands between my knees to stop them shaking. "I took this and the box I found in my house to Arthur Mackie. He said the photos are of his sister Alice and brother Vincent. Father Murphy also gave me some old photos of the mill, one of a girl who lived there called Dorothy Killigrew." Alice's lips pursed, but she held my gaze. "It's like building a puzzle without the picture," I said. "Lots of pieces but I don't quite know where they fit."

"You're tenacious, to say the least," Alice said.

I'd reached a point of no return. I had to know. "Are you Arthur's sister, Alice?"

She smiled. "Yes. I am she."

I touched the pendant beneath my shirt. Questions hammered in my head. "I had no idea."

"And no reason why you should," she said. "Last time we bumped into each other Felicity whisked me off before I could introduce myself."

"Ben knew," I said, "yet he didn't say anything." Another layer of deceit.

Colette's phone buzzed. She excused herself and closed the hallway door behind her. Through the dappled glass panes, I watched her hover in the entrance.

"I've been waiting for you to come with your questions," Alice said. "Felicity went berserk when you started digging. She knew you'd uncover the truth, and she's such a protective little thing. She swore Ben and the rest of us to secrecy."

"But why? If everyone knows then what's there to hide?"

She ran her nails along her scalp and swept a strand of hair behind her ear. "It's not so much the secrecy. She thinks she's protecting me. When you and Ben became an item, she realised the implications and set about splitting you apart." She held up a finger. "But before you judge her, that protection extends to you too. If Dorothy's curse is to be believed, then you are at risk."

"Dorothy's curse?" I'd upgraded from haunted house.

"I'd like to see the family tree you've constructed," Alice said. "I could help you fill in the blanks."

I glanced at the door. "Do you have time?"

Her laugh crackled. "I have nothing but time. Stick your head out and tell Letty to bring the family bible."

I cracked the door and caught Colette's eye. "Alice wants the family bible."

She gave a feeble laugh. "Of course she does."

The three of us huddled around Colette's dining table, the colossal family bible's back pages open for inspection, and my notebook laid out between us. Alice perched her specs on the end of her nose and traced a fingertip from entry to entry, nodding or shaking her head as she went. "Not a bad attempt," she said.

Colette recited names from the Bible's penned list whilst Alice struck out or ticked my entries and added some of her own. "Alice Mackie, blah blah blah, married James Marshall, first of November nineteen fifty-two."

I smiled. "I heard you were a full moon bride."

Alice's face beamed. "They called me Mrs Moonshine."

"Agnes Eden told me."

"She and her sister Lucy were my bridesmaids. God, that's forever ago." Her eyes glistened. "Next."

In brackets alongside James Marshall's name the inscription read (died peacefully, 18th April 1989).

"Eleanor Marshall, born fifth of May nineteen fifty-eight."

"My daughter." Alice said.

Colette's eyebrows twitched. "Married Gordon Shaw, seventh of June nineteen eighty."

"Ellie passed away on New Year's Day, two thousand and one." Alice and Colette stared at the entry alongside Eleanor's name, each lost in their own memory.

"Then Felicity and Ben," Alice said. She grinned at Colette, "And you're our baby, thrice blessed."

"Penny's the baby," Colette said.

"You'll always be my little grandbaby."

Colette made a mock eye roll and closed the bible.

"There, you've got our branch." Alice underlined Dorothy Killigrew's name. "Now yours. Start with George and Gladys, and their sons Arthur and Vincent."

"How are they my relatives?"

"Ah. So . . ." She drew a dotted line from Vincent to Dorothy and another dotted line from Vincent to herself. She underlined Vincent and enclosed his name in brackets. ". . . Arthur married May Errington in nineteen forty-three. They had a daughter, Georgina."

I recalled the baptism entry in the church's register. She drew a line from Arthur to May, then wrote Georgina.

"Georgie married Freddy, your grandfather. She lost her first baby, but they went on and had two sons, your father Byron, and William." Alice connected James and Frederick Marshall with a solid line and scribbled 'brothers' beneath.

She wrote Bill's name next to my father's and connected them with a line, and added Shelly's name as Sean, above Bill's.

"Byron married Rachel," Alice said, "and gave us your lovely little face." She pinched my cheek between her fingers, and we giggled.

"Can I ask you something else?"

Alice's eyes widened and a smile twitched at the corner of her mouth. "Yes, of course."

"Gladys Hendry died when you were a baby, so who raised you?"

She clapped. "You're perceptive." She flipped through the bible and extracted a sepia photograph of a dark-haired woman with sallow features, and a staid vicar, and between them a pram with the biggest wheels I'd ever seen. "My grandmother. Elise Killigrew. The mill fire left her homeless, and George Mackie needed a housekeeper." She winked. "They came to a convenient arrangement and eventually married."

I had the missing pieces to my puzzle. I'd found

Dorothy's mother. And her daughter. I slid the pendant out from beneath my shirt. "Did this belong to Dorothy?"

Alice beamed. "Yes. Elise didn't salvage much from the fire, but the pendant survived. I gave it to you because I thought it might act as a talisman and keep you safe."

"From Dorothy?"

"Yes." Alice shifted the notebook. She extended a line from Rachel and wrote Gareth, then drew another dotted line and added Tracy. She drew a circle around Tracy, Felicity, Rachel and Georgina and underlined my name. "Now you have your full picture."

"What's the circles?"

"Dorothy's curse," Alice said. "Extending from Gladys." She ran a finger from Gladys Hendry through the circled names. "All had the wrong bloodline and the misfortune of stepping on Dorothy's domain."

My heart fluttered. "Why Felicity? She's on your side."

Alice nodded. "It took us a while to figure out. Turns out Tom has Errington blood on his mother's side."

"He's related to Arthur's wife."

"Yep. Though there's no direct bloodline, it's the only connection we could make."

"Unless Dorothy doesn't care who she hurts," Colette said.

My stomach gurgled with trapped hysteria. Dorothy's daughter sat next to me making casual conversation about her mother's psychotic curse. And me? The thought of being related to Gladys Hendry made me feel sick. I couldn't have made this shit up if I'd tried.

"Gran?" Colette tapped the bible's cover. "Everyone Dorothy's attacked has been pregnant, right?"

Alice nodded. Her eyes slid to me and the corners crinkled.

"Then why is she making Veronica's life hell?"

"Veronica's at the end of a long line, it seems," Alice said. "She's kind of brought this full circle."

Colette straightened and looked at me. Blood drained from her face and her jaw dropped. "Does Ben know?" She eyed my belly. "You shouldn't be living in that house. He of all people knows the danger you're in."

I shrugged. "I have nowhere else to go. I've put everything I own into the house. For the first time in my life I'm out of my mother's control and now a ghost wants to push me around."

"Not just for your sake." Alice placed a hand over mine. "But for your baby. When I say you've come full circle, I mean your baby has both Mackie and Killigrew blood running through its veins."

"But your branch does too," I said.

"No." Alice pointed at Vincent's name. "My father was a Mackie in name only. George and Gladys adopted him as a baby from a dishonoured young cousin of hers."

"Oh my God, that's what Filly meant," Colette said. "She said if Veronica and Ben. . ."

The room's heat was suffocating.

Alice sighed. "Your and Ben's baby closes the loop."

I sat back and studied the tapestry of names in front of me. When I'd first come to the hamlet and seen the house for sale the pull had been undeniable. I had a vivid memory of that day. I'd come to Cornwall to see where my father had grown up, and I found my home. Before I'd contacted the agent, and before I'd looked inside, I knew the house belonged to me.

I had found my home, and it had found me. I followed the line Alice had drawn between the circled names. This horror had begun with Dorothy and Gladys, and now she intended to end her legacy of destruction with me.

CHAPTER 25

I SIGNED OFF AN EMAIL TO MY EDITOR, attached my article, and clicked send. Two down, one to go. I'd found my work mojo despite Dorothy's constant interference. My phone's alarm pinged. I donned my snow boots, cocooned myself in jacket and scarf, locked the front door and tugged my beanie over my ears. Winter sun glinted off puddles of snow melt and an icy breeze swept the sky clear of clouds.

I waved at Father Murphy mopping the church steps, and scanned the pub's car park. The nearer I got, the harder my heart pounded. Lunch with my mother, after a week of silence, meant she'd be leaving at last.

"Sit down." Rachel sat upright, ankles crossed, and plucked at a thread on her sleeve. Around us the pub's sparse clientele huddled in corners and against radiators, and meaty aromas wafted from their laden plates. Kenver manned the lunch shift solo, no sign of Shelly.

I obeyed. I wouldn't have to wait long for a snipe. Hives tingled at the base of my neck and her silence unnerved me.

"I'm going home, Roo," she said. "The roads are clear so there's no point staying, but I don't want to leave with this horrible cloud hanging over us."

Here it came.

"I suppose what happened was inevitable." she said. "You've always been out of control and now you've made your bed. I've done my best to give you a stable upbringing. You've wanted for nothing, and you destroyed a perfectly good marriage."

At least her insults remained consistent. "Do you hear yourself?" I said. "You say you don't want to leave under a cloud, but then you just pile on the abuse. It's time to let the past go, mother."

She scoffed. "Your father would be disappointed to see what's become of you."

Always her tactic when an argument failed. Conjure a negative image of my father, his blood matted beard, torn lips and sightless eyes. Pain infused every fibre and cell in my body. I took a long, deep breath. "Would he?" She jutted her jaw and studied my face. I refused to give her the reaction she expected.

Before she could retaliate, Ben pushed his way through the doors, spotted us, and walked across. She shifted in her chair and clasped her hands on the table. Repressed fury turned her knuckles white.

"Ladies?" He removed his beanie and bent to kiss my cheek. "Can I get you some drinks?" He winked at me, "Or a coffee?"

"Tea for me. I'm driving," Rachel said. Her eyes never left my face and she waited until Ben was out of earshot. "You've got yourself a real winner this time. I've heard all about him and his antics."

"Of course you have," I said. "You've had too many cosy pyjama parties with your brother's whore wife. Did you tell her all my secrets too? Did you build her a picture of how unstable I am so she can share her knowledge with the community?"

She barked. "You've painted the unstable picture all by yourself, Roo. You don't need me for that."

Ben returned with a pint of beer. Kenver followed with my coffee and a pot of tea for Rachel. "Are you ladies lunching?"

The thought of food turned my guts. "No. My mother's leaving."

Rachel smirked. "And not soon enough."

Hats off to Ben, he'd either prepared himself for a standoff, or had become desensitised to our bickering. "The weather's expected to hold so you should have a good trip," he said.

Her eyes slid from him to me, like a huntress feline with ears pressed flat against her head, stalking, crouched to pounce. "So, Ben, do you plan to make an honest woman of my daughter? I hear you're quite the gentleman."

"You shouldn't believe everything you hear," he said. He gulped his beer and glanced at me.

"Well, since you're unlikely to see me around here again," Rachel said, "perhaps I should remind you, you'll have your hands full with this one."

Ben nodded. He reached and took hold of my hand. "I expect so, Rachel."

My eyes conveyed a silent message. Please don't tell her.

"When her father died she fell to pieces." Rachel stirred her tea and tapped the teaspoon against the cup. "The whole world had to come to a standstill so she could suck up sympathy and wallow in pity."

"Mother." I shrugged off Ben's hand. I needed air.

"Oh, the drama. Nobody else got a word in edgeways for her screaming and performing."

Ben gripped my elbow. "It's all right. Let's get it all out in the open and then she's got nothing left."

Rachel laughed. "You're mistaken. I have plenty. Years and years of stories I can tell. You'll not get a moment's peace with her, I promise you."

"Enough." I shoved my chair back and wrangled with my jacket sleeves.

Ben caught my hand. "You need to let her do this. Don't walk away and give her power over you."

"It's not about power," Rachel said. "It's about exorcising a demon. My demon." She looked at me. "You."

Defeated, I sank into my chair.

"I wish you had died in the crash." Rachel banged a fist on the table. "I'd rather have lost both of you than live with what's left of you."

Ben's face lost its semblance of disinterest.

"When the paramedics reached them, Ruth clung to her father. She wouldn't let go. She screamed. She yelled all the way to hospital, and she screamed the roof off the emergency room until they sedated her."

I lowered my head and fiddled with my zipper. I slid the little hard bit into the runner and raised the zip tooth by tooth. Strobing blue lights, the sickening smell of coolant and burnt rubber, and blood, the screech of tearing metal and clattering gurneys played through my mind on a loop, repressed memories revived.

"They had to section her," Rachel said. "No one could get through to her with all her screaming and performing and hair tearing. I had to bury my husband and deal with her self-pity. I had no time to grieve. No time for me to come to terms with my loss."

Ben glanced at me. I swallowed bitter bile.

"But we got through it. I focused all my attention on her, on getting her better. When Graeme came along, I thought we'd finally arrived at a good place. But no, not to be." She downed the last of her tea. Her cup clattered in its saucer. "She had everything. The best psychiatrist. A loving husband. She didn't have to lift a finger."

"Graeme was not a loving husband, and you know it."

Rachel inhaled, pressed her lips together, and shook

her head.

"You had one job, to keep him happy. He'd not have strayed if you were capable of a tiny bit of warmth."

Ben signalled to Kenver for another pint of beer.

I glared at her. "As for your shrink buddy Huey . . ."

"Heyworth." Rachel corrected. "For God's sake Ruth."

I chuckled. Unchecked hysteria made me warm and heady. "Yeah, him. Ask him about the times he put his hand on my leg, ran his fingers under my skirt whilst trying to convince me he had the answer to all my problems."

Rachel's mouth opened for a shocked intake of breath. "You little swine."

"Oh, sorry." I feigned surprise. "I remember now, he was screwing you at the time."

She smacked the teapot, which slid across the table, toppled and spilt hot tea into my lap. Ben snatched the pot and hoicked me out the chair. I doubled over and bayed in an ugly half howl, half laugh. I wanted to scream. I wanted to rip her hair out of her fucking head.

"I've had enough of you two." Ben slammed the pot onto the table, attracting looks from Kenver and the remaining punters. He lifted my handbag off the floor and caught my elbow. "Have a safe trip, Rachel. I can't say it was a pleasure meeting you and I hope I never see you again."

Her expression of disgust shredded my resolve. My legs trembled and tears blinded me. I would never tell her about my baby, never let her darkness infect my child the way she'd polluted my life with her despicable hatred.

Kenver nodded as Ben and I passed the bar, and once outside I let out a sob.

Ben held me. "Sorry, I've been an idiot. Come home with me?"

"You won't be able to stay here once the baby comes," Shelly stretched her legs across Ben's sofa. "It's pokey. You need room."

"I don't mind, at least for the first year or so. It's not like there's a lot of property choice around here. Ben's mentioned moving away, but we'll see."

"Some locals were talking in the pub about your house being for sale," Shelly said. "There's a sweepstake to see how long it takes to sell."

I laughed. "Did you place a bet?"

"Well yeah," she said. "I guessed at never."

"Ben wants me moved in by month end, so I've made arrangements to put my furniture into storage and then I'll decide what to do with everything once this is all over." I stroked my belly's slight swell.

"Why wait? Move in and sort everything out as you go? It's not like much is going to change in a couple of weeks."

"If I leave the house empty someone might break in."

Shelly's eyebrows disappeared beneath her fringe.

"Good luck to them, don't you think, with your state of the art security."

"True." I studied her face. Her fringe had grown but some silvery scars remained on her forehead. She visited whenever I stayed over at Ben's, otherwise I didn't get to see much of her outside the pub. She'd dropped in after lunch with foil wrapped sandwiches and we'd had a lounge picnic.

"Anyway, I'm off. Say hi to lover boy." She got to her feet, straightened her skirt and puckered her lips to kiss my cheek. "Love you. Stay here or make sure Ben's with you when you go to the house."

I made a false promise. Dorothy's activity had ramped up a notch since I'd started showing and I found it harder to control my fear. Late afternoon I let myself out through the garden gate. Ben had a job to finish in Falmouth, so I had the night to myself. I lay a handful of daffodils on Vincent's grave and cut across the churchyard avoiding the front doors and the possibility of bumping into Father Murphy.

Inside the house a cold staleness greeted me. I dropped my keys on the coffee table and boosted the heating. Silence. Sound died inside my house. At Ben's I could always hear cars passing, or a dog bark, and birdsong.

I made a mug of tea and selected his number from my contacts.

"What's up?"

"I'm at home," I said. "I thought I'd stop in tonight and do some packing while you're away."

The heaviness in his silence spoke for itself.

"I'll be fine. It's just one night." I didn't want Ben's crankiness to rub off on me. The house still belonged to me. "I'm a big girl."

"Anything so much as creaks and you leave, please."

I swallowed a mouthful of hot tea. "I will. Promise. See you tomorrow." I ended the call and as I climbed the stairs I fished the pendant out from beneath my shirt. Alice's talisman. I touched the stone for luck.

By midnight I'd packed my office and bedroom and crammed most of my clothes into a suitcase. The rest went into boxes. I made a final round of upstairs and turned off the lights, a kind of reverse motion to the day I moved in. My chest ached from exertion and sadness.

I settled on the sofa, my bedding nested around me, and dozed, semi-conscious of the fridge's mechanical hum, radiators ticking as they cooled, and my heart's rhythmic pulse. Soft at first, a cat meowled. Then more urgent, a cry, a snort then a high-pitched wail. Not a cat, a baby's cry. I tugged the duvet over my head and curled into myself, at my core my baby's soft swell.

Upstairs, the wail became a whimper.

I waited; my breath laboured beneath the covers. I touched the pendant at my throat. At a run, I'd reach the front door in four steps. I folded back the duvet and lifted my keys and phone off the coffee table.

Moonlight glinted off the kitchen door handle as it swung and slammed. Every door in the house banged, one after another, and around me the darkness screamed.

CHAPTER 26

I STOOD BENEATH THE MAGNOLIA TREE'S TWISTED LIMBS. A sparkle of sunlight flashed between branches thick with buds and flowers, and along the garden wall the rhododendrons frothed with blossoms. The spring breeze's subtle fragrance transformed the air and gave the woods a breath of life.

A blanket of bluebells covered the ground from the mill ruin all the way to the rag tree, and shrill birdsong erupted from the trees in my garden and the woodlands beyond. My house stood empty. Lacked the thrill of burgeoning life. Much had happened in the five months since I'd moved in, so much in such a short time.

I inhaled the crisp floral scented air. On fine days it seemed like the winter had been nothing more than a bad dream. My phone vibrated. Ben. Alice had fallen during the night and he and his sisters had followed the ambulance to hospital. "Are you still at the house?"

"Yeah. The removal van's just left. I'm going to tidy and I'll be home in about an hour. How's Alice?"

"They're keeping her in. Looks like a fractured hip."

"I'm so sorry for her. Will you be staying?"

"As soon as we know what ward they're sending her to we'll head home. Don't cook, I'll get something on the way."

"Send my love if you see her."

"I will," he said. "Don't hang around that place."

"I won't." The sunshine lent the house a benign aspect. I glanced across at the jagged stump where the tree which had crushed my roof once stood. I traced the path, now almost hidden between new growth and trees, where Vincent had trod. A cold chill touched my neck and I shuddered.

I locked the kitchen door and dropped the key into the cutlery drawer. My short stay had done nothing to influence the room's unpleasant sterility and resonance.

The doorbell pealed a repetitive impatient Morse code. I checked the time. Shelly's shift didn't finish till four, and she wouldn't come to the house regardless. I hadn't arranged to meet anyone else. I edged past the window and spotted Tracy's car on the drive. Shit. I swung open the door.

"You going to invite me in?" White teeth sliced her cherry lips in half. I stepped aside and let her pass. Her perfume wafted in my face, spice and incense. She sauntered through the unfurnished space, her heel taps loud in the emptiness. She crossed her arms over her chest and swivelled to face me.

"What do you want?" I adjusted my cardigan to conceal my waistline from her intrusive gaze.

"I know what you think of me," she said, pasting on a smirk. "You've always judged me because your husband couldn't keep his hands and dick to himself."

"Or maybe because of the way you treat your own husband." And your persistence with Ben.

She ignored me. "Ben and I are different," she said, as if she'd read my mind. "We have something special. We've got a long history and you don't get to walk in here and make a grab at him because he paid you a bit of attention. I've told you he's taken, but you like getting your own way, don't you, Ruth?"

I almost pitied her attempt to remind me of my own faults.

"Whatever you think you have with him, it's nothing. That baby's not going to keep him. He'll soon be sick of playing house with you." She paced, tramped the scorched floorboards, her posture rigid.

"What went wrong between you and Gareth?" I said.

She lowered her arms and her hands dangled at her sides. Her nail tips susurrated against her trousers. Her mouth twisted and her chest heaved. "None of your business, you stupid bitch."

I'd touched a nerve. "Do you think he deserves to be

treated like this? He's stuck by you through everything. He loves you."

"This is not about him." She shrieked, and spit flew from her mouth. She cleared the distance between us and stabbed a finger into my chest. "Or you."

I collided with the wall. "Tracy, pull yourself together."

Her forehead almost touched mine. Her pupils dilated and I smelled stale alcohol on her breath. "You think your baby is going to survive this?" She waved her arm. "It won't. And all you'll get for your trouble is his pity. He doesn't love you and he doesn't want your baby."

Her words cut deep. "This is his baby too," I said. "Maybe it's time you let go of him. Jealousy is clouding your judgement." I pushed past her and aimed for the door. She lashed out before I'd taken two steps. One hand clasped my arm and the other clawed my face.

I shrugged free of her grasp and earned a hard smack across my ear which cracked my head off the wall. Her next swing caught me on my nose and bright berries of blood dropped onto the front of my t-shirt.

"Stop it. Jesus Tracy, what the hell?" She lunged at me and I retreated. My ankle twisted and I hit the floor on my backside. She teetered over me and grabbed a handful of my hair. I clamped her wrists and twisted onto my knees to get out of her grip.

The ceiling creaked. The distraction earned me a second and I got to my feet. She grinned. "Told you." She turned and bolted up the stairs.

"Don't go up." I eyed the front door and considered my options. I couldn't leave her. I followed her, took the stairs two at a time, and stopped on the mid landing. The air shimmered and stank of sulphur and smoke. Static crackled and lifted the ends of my hair. The shoe box's contents littered the landing. Impossible. I'd returned everything to Alice. Penny must have snuck in behind the removal men to set up her prank. Little shit.

I climbed to Tracy's level. "We need to get out of here." Gall rose in my throat as the signet ring, buttons and coins skittered across the floor like they'd been tossed by an angry hand. In my bedroom doorway the baby's photo rocked on its stand and flew at us with tremendous force.

The frame caught the corner of Tracy's eyebrow. She lost her footing and collapsed into me. The impact knocked the air out of my lungs, and we crouched on the stairs. "We have to get out of here." I coughed out strings of spit and blood. She elbowed her arm out of my grip and took another swipe at me.

The pack of letters lay on the carpet next to the photograph. The ribbon which bound the bundle blackened and unfurled and the envelope corners curled and smoked as flames ignited the paper.

Tracy clutched the banister, her nails torn, eyes fixed on the flaming envelopes. Blood trickled down her cheek. In that moment, between realisation and action, in the calm silence before the tempest, she looked at me. Her eyes focused and slid to my belly. She tilted her head and laughed. "I thought I'd give Dorothy a helping hand."

Smoke percolated across the ceiling. Flames caught and spread over the carpet and lapped the skirting boards. I grasped her wrist. "What have you done? We've got to get out. Now."

She slapped my hand away and we retreated to the mid landing. A blast of hot air struck us and slammed us against the banister. Tracy clung to the spindles, her grin replaced by a rictus of horror. Below, flames climbed the walls, and a lava flow of fire consumed the varnished floor.

My flesh and hair seared. I touched my belly. Dorothy was not going to take my baby. I scrammed up the stairs into the bathroom and twisted the cold tap open. Water spluttered and gushed into the bath. I yanked my forgotten robe off the door hook, climbed into the tub, and shoved it under the flow.

Above the fire's roar came a rhythmic thump, like someone banged on a door. My eyes and nose streamed. I kneeled and soaked my hair under the tap then bundled the robe under my arm. I returned to Tracy and draped the robe over us.

We huddled on the landing. Noise and indecision drowned out rational thought. We had minutes before the robe dried and combusted. Tracy's eyes bugged but she refused to move. I gripped her shoulders and shook her. "If we don't move, we're going to burn to death."

Burn to death, like Dorothy.

"*Roo . . .*"

Icy dread quelled the heat in my veins. I glanced up. Dorothy stood on the top step, a dark ravaged figure engulfed in flames and coils of acrid black smoke. Her dark hair floated around her atrophied face and shoulders.

I straightened. The robe fell away, and Tracy fastened a hand around my ankle. "What the hell are you doing?"

I faced Dorothy. Time slowed. Flames and sparks whirled around her. Her shadowed eyes, ruined by death and hatred, held mine. "Let us go, please?" I sobbed. My tears dried before they could fall. I lay a hand over the swell of my stomach. "I'm sorry for what happened to you, but my baby is innocent. We have your blood. We're part of you. Please, don't do this?"

She extended her withered arm and held the polka dot scarf out to me. The staircase creaked and shuddered as fire consumed the timber frame. I caught the scarf's frayed end, shoved the silk bundle into my pocket and turned to lift Tracy. I covered our heads with the robe and I didn't look back. "Run."

We leaped down the stairs as the upper flight dislodged in a spume of sparks and smoke. My shoes sank into the flames and the leather scorched and blackened. Tracy's sandals offered no protection. The hems of her trousers ignited.

"Oh God." My lips blistered. "It's like walking on coals, just keep moving." She wailed and slumped against me. "No. Don't you dare stop, we're almost there." Daylight glinted beyond the dark smoke and flames. Somewhere glass shattered. I adjusted my shoulder to support her and scratched around the drawer for the backdoor key.

The robe slipped and I lurched. The key fell and skittered across the floor. Tracy's feet were black and blistered, and flames climbed her trousers. She vomited and her legs gave way. I crouched beneath her and supported her knees. "You're going to be okay, you hear me." I lifted her onto the worktop and pushed her legs up after her. "We have to get the window open." I gripped the taps and heaved myself onto the counter. Shelly stood on the grass outside. She waved her arms, her mouth wide in a toneless scream. Her makeup had run and made panda eyes.

I felt around for something, anything, to break the glass. Every breath I took burnt deeper into my lungs. I sprawled across the sink and kicked at the soot-coated glass. No air. Shelly's face contorted. She pressed her hands into her mouth and crouched on the grass.

Ben and Gareth arrived at the window as the staircase collapsed. A fireball exploded through the kitchen door. Ben caught Shelly's elbow and dragged her across the garden. The window shattered and flames engulfed me before the cold air could touch my face.

CHAPTER 27

DARK SOOTY CLOUDS OBSCURED THE SKY and tiny fireflies swirled higher and higher until they disappeared from sight. The air and ground thrummed, and voices and shadowed forms drifted through the haze. I lay on a sheet, half on my side, one of my legs hooked beneath me. Water sprayed over me in gentle swooping arcs, like my dad used to do with the hosepipe on hot summer days.

I squeezed my eyes and my lids stuck together.

The voices around me made no sense.

A crash, and shouts, dragged me from oblivion. I sucked in short breaths. Mucus clogged my throat and I retched. I raised my head and coughed. I cried, but no sound escaped apart from gurgles and threads of mucus laced with the iron bitterness of blood.

"Ben, help her." Shelly's shout cut through the thrum.

A shadow loomed. I couldn't focus through the fatty

goo which stuck my eyelids together.

"Veronica?"

Ben? I raised my head. I braced my hands and feet to shove myself up, except my limbs wouldn't cooperate and I collapsed.

"Keep spraying." Ben shouted. His voice dropped. "Lie still. I'm right here."

Shelly sobbed. "I'm spraying, for fuck sake. Where's the ambulance? Help her."

Their voices receded, garbled curses and nonsensical words.

"Veronica?" A woman spoke. "I'm going to pour water over your eyes. Do you understand?"

I croaked. Cool water splashed over my face. I gasped and lashed out.

"Try and keep still. The water will soothe the pain. Can you do that for me?"

I cried, more a visceral howl. Water spilled over my eyes and into my mouth. A spasm racked my body and I coughed and retched.

"You're doing fine, Veronica. Keep taking breaths."

"Ben?" I couldn't get enough air into my lungs.

"I'm here." He sounded strange.

"Veronica." The woman's shadow leaned across me. "I'm going to give you oxygen. You'll feel a pressure over your nose and mouth."

I raised a hand to my face. A gentle touch on my wrist lowered my arm to my side. "Keep still. You're doing great."

A new voice. "We're ready to move her."

"Veronica, in a minute we're going to lift you. First we'll turn you and then we'll make the transition as quick as we can."

Despite the grit and gunk which gummed my eyelashes together, I had partial vision over the top of the oxygen mask. Nearby, soggy charred rags lay in a heap on the grass.

"Keep still," the woman said.

"What's happening?" I struggled onto an elbow.

"Don't," Ben leaned over me. "Lie still, please."

The woman placed a hand behind my head. She counted, three, two, and with a swift manoeuvre I lay on my back. I turned my head.

A few feet from me paramedics huddled over a grey shape. Gareth kneeled beside them, his face crumpled, his mouth contorted. Scattered across the grass lay bits of burnt rag, and my scorched robe.

Oh God.

"Jesus, Tracy." I snatched the mask off, attempted to roll onto my knees and flailed as several pairs of hands pinned me down.

Shelly screamed. Ben placed a hand in the centre of my chest. I thrashed and howled. The woman gripped my shoulders. "Veronica, look at me. I need you to concentrate on my voice. Look at me." I couldn't tear my eyes away from Tracy's lifeless body.

A paramedic ran towards us with a stretcher.

A keening gurgle clogged my throat. The woman replaced the oxygen mask. "We're going to lift you now," she said. She glanced at Ben. "Hold her head still as you can."

His face distorted. "Where are you taking her?"

My cries drowned her reply, then treetops and sky moved above me and blank faces peered from the edges of my vision.

Shelly ran beside me, her face a smudge of mascara and tears.

Light and sound faded.

I swallowed, and gagged on a mouthful of plastic.

"I'm right here," Ben said.

No air. I couldn't breathe.

I couldn't lift myself. The effort to move sent my body into a spasm.

Tears leaked out the corners of my eyes.

Pinpricks of light flickered like teeny stars in a midnight sky.

A scuffle. "Stand clear."

The starlight engulfed me and faded into darkness.

"Please, stay with me." Ben's strangled voice came from miles away.

"Clear."

Starlight exploded in my head and chest. The heat inside me flared, burned, and cooled.

Silence.

Ben's breath warmed my ear. "I love you, always."

Chapter 28

Of all days to be late.

My mother's car pulled alongside the curb. She parked and alighted, straightened the creases in her coat and crossed the road.

Sunlight filtered through branches and leaves and cast a dappled mosaic on the ground. I glanced around, surprised by the number of people gathered beneath the rag tree's canopy.

Colette stood silent beside Ben, her arm around his waist. Both looked as though they'd rather be someplace else. Felicity, Tom and Gareth huddled with their heads bowed in conversation.

My mother took hold of Shelly's hand, and they navigated the roots until they stood beneath the tree's branches, sparse of leaves but clothed in a colourful array of ribbons and fabrics.

In the sunshine the tree's tokens appeared almost beautiful.

Alice stood silent, hands folded in front of her, a smile on her lips and a faraway look in her pale eyes.

Father Murphy threaded his way through the crowd and cleared his throat. Voices hushed. Birds twittered and fluttered overhead. I skirted the group and made my way towards Ben and Colette. "Thank you all for making the journey here today," Father Murphy said. "I greet you, not only as a priest but as a friend of the families on whose behalf this blessing will be conducted."

I caught Shelly's eye and waved. She blew her nose, tucked the tissue in her pocket and hooked her arm through my mother's. They turned to face Ben. Both seemed wan, and my mother lacked her typical arrogance.

From his pocket, Ben lifted out Dorothy's frayed and charred polka dot scarf and tied it around the branch next to Vincent's tie. Together, if not in life, then at least in a symbolic partnership.

Alice stepped away from my side. A ray of sunlight touched her and she glowed with an ethereal beauty. Penny beamed at her and held out her hand. "Come, Nan."

Colette unfurled a lavender ribbon, reached into the tree, and tied a floppy bow. She mopped her tears and Felicity wrapped her arms around her and rocked with her as she sobbed.

I reached Ben's side. A sun beam caught on a dewdrop and cast a miniature rainbow within the microcosm. I'd spent so much time hating the tree that I hadn't taken time to notice its true beauty. Every rag, ribbon and token possessed an aura, a pulse of energy which transmitted a musical tinkle, like a thousand chimes dancing on the breeze.

Gareth nodded at Ben and stepped forward, features drawn and shoulders slouched. He stretched to a naked limb, bowed the wood and fastened a strip of white floral fabric, looped through a gold band, to the branch. He swiped a hand across his eyes. "I loved my Tracy more than life."

Felicity dabbed a tissue at the corners of her eyes then blew her nose.

"She's here." Penny touched Ben's elbow and grinned at me.

Ben turned and whispered. "Veronica?"

"Yes." I linked my arm through his and looked at Penny. "What's going on?"

She pressed a finger to her lips. "Listen."

Everyone looked at us. Shelly placed a shaky hand over her mouth and hiccupped. My mother stared at Ben, expressionless, the corners of her mouth drooped. Tears dropped and bloomed on her coat.

Ben sighed. He opened his fist and the pendant Alice had given me lay in his palm. He faced me. He cut his eyes to Penny and she nodded. "I love you," he said. "I loved you from the moment I first saw you. We had everything to live for . . . our baby. . ."

I lay a hand over my flat stomach.

Shelly sobbed into her hands. I studied the faces around me. Except for Penny, nobody made eye contact. Not one person could bear to look at me. Not even Father Murphy.

I glanced at Ben. He wound the gold chain around his finger and raised his arm between the branches. He hooked the chain on a splinter and the sunlight glinted off the dangling pendant.

Father Murphy raised his hand. "Eternal rest grant unto them, O Lord, and let perpetual light shine upon them. May the souls of the faithful departed through the mercy of God rest in peace. Amen."

The crowd muttered amen.

Few of us remained beneath the trees. My mother argued with Ben and Colette. Shelly paced, arms wrapped around herself, her heels clogged with mud. Felicity and Tom comforted Gareth.

The tree's tokens fluttered. Alice touched my hand. She pointed to the lavender bow. "I wore that at Colette's christening. She was a beautiful baby. Always was my favourite." She lowered her arm and sighed.

One by one they left.

Penny picked her way across the tree's roots and turned to wave. Colette looked over at me. I waved back. Then they too were gone.

Ben paced, hands in his pockets. He leaned against

the tree's trunk and stared up at my pendant. Clouds scudded across the sun and I shivered. He buried his face in his hands and wept.

For weeks following the blessing, Ben and Gareth worked at a relentless pace to clear away the house's rubble. They dug down to the foundations and carted away stone, brick, metal and wire until they'd removed every last trace of house and mill.

Locals came and went, offered moral support, shook their heads and scratched their chins. Passers-by looked the other way. Dog walkers crossed to the opposite side of the road.

Winter storms raged. Spring blossomed. Easter passed and the ground dried out. Gareth graded and landscaped the property and Ben seeded grass and wildflowers between the trees.

One bright summer morning, familiar faces converged and Father Murphy consecrated the ground.

Ben lined Vincent's path through the trees with small white stones and filled the track with gravel, a permanent short cut to our shrine.

I couldn't remember a more beautiful summer. I sat on one of the three new benches cemented into a triangle beneath the magnolia tree whilst Ben cleared weeds from a flower bed. One day, perhaps years from now when memories faded, our garden of remembrance would hear children's laughter, and visitors would sit beneath the tree's branches and reflect.

A car stopped at the curb. Ben dusted his hands, shaded his eyes, and watched Penny skip across the grass, a floral bouquet in her arms. She gave him a wave and flopped onto the bench beside me, breathless, lanky legs stuck out in front of her. "Do you like the flowers I've brought you?"

Author's Note

The Pagan Tree was inspired by a visit to the eerie and unsettling Munlochy Clootie Well on the Black Isle in Scotland. Rag trees and clootie wells exist in woodlands throughout Scotland, Ireland and England. Pilgrimages to these sites hark back to pre-Christian traditions of placing cloth offerings to nature spirits and goddesses living in and around wells and springs to honour them or to seek cures from illness by tying rags to the branches of surrounding trees. With the arrival of Christianity, the number of wells diminished and these pagan traditions were frowned upon. However, whilst the Christian church adopted many well sites and named them after their saints, the practice of leaving cloth and votive offerings, including religious icons and other symbols of faith, continued. To this day, pilgrimages to clootie wells are popular, especially during the Gaelic festivals of Imbolc, Beltane, Lughnasadh, or Samhain.

Acknowledgements

Thanks Mom for surrounding me with the books I grew up with, which filled my head with endless adventures and fuelled my imagination.

Thank you to my wonderful husband Rob for essential tea top-ups and for bearing silent witness to my story ideas, character conundrums and plot holes, detailed accounts of horror and hauntings, and especially for believing in me.

To my bestie Jan, for alpha reading my first draft, and to Jasmin for critiquing my cover and beta reading my manuscript, thank you to both of you for your unwavering support and for regularly dragging me out of my bottomless pit of self-doubt.

Special thanks to Helen Bowman of In The Detail for proofreading my manuscript, to James and Becky Wright of Platform House Publishing for designing The Pagan Tree's cover, and to Julia Scott, Evenstar Books, for formatting and adding the final touches to my book.

Printed in Great Britain
by Amazon

37807649R00145